NOV 0 1 2012

Stream Runner

FOUR WINDS PRESS   NEW YORK

David Seed

Stream
Runner

To Jack and Huldah

LIBRARY OF CONGRESS CATALOGING IN PUBLICATION DATA

Seed, David.
    Stream runner.

    SUMMARY: Leif Collins is in no hurry to grow up as he enjoys trout fishing and swimming with his friends in his northern California town.
    [1. Fishing—Fiction.   2. Friendship—Fiction]
I. Title.
PZ7.S4512St   [Fic]   78–21769
ISBN 0–590–07568–3

Published by Four Winds Press
A division of Scholastic Magazines, Inc., New York, N.Y.
Copyright © 1979 by David Seed
All rights reserved
Printed in the United States of America
Library of Congress Catalog Card Number: 78–21769
1   2   3   4   5   83   82   81   80   79

"Time is but the stream I go a-fishing in."

—Henry David Thoreau

1

The morning was bright but still cool when I woke up the first time, and I savored the pleasing realization that I didn't have to get up to go to school. I lay stretched out on my stomach. One arm was crooked over my head while the other dangled off the bed. My head was on the edge of the mattress.

I heard birds chirping in the old black walnut tree next to the bedroom window. Then I made out the sounds of pigeons cooing. The loft was in a shed on the other side of the garage. I opened my eyes slowly and found myself looking at Thor's bed which was against the opposite wall.

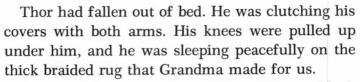

Thor had fallen out of bed. He was clutching his covers with both arms. His knees were pulled up under him, and he was sleeping peacefully on the thick braided rug that Grandma made for us.

I guessed that no one heard Thor fall out of bed. We were always hearing Thor go thump on the floor and having to run in and lift him back into bed. I hadn't fallen out of bed myself since I was nine years old. Most of the time I hadn't known anything about it, because someone put me back; but I remembered waking up on the floor a couple of times. I guessed that for once Thor was going to wake up on the floor, because I wasn't about to get up and put him back in bed.

Anyhow Thor would have something to talk about. He had just learned to talk well, and he chattered constantly. He seemed to think that he knew everything. I got my stiff arm down from over my head and managed to roll over to the center of my bed. I pulled a sheet up over me and dozed off again into the luxury of sleep.

2

The morning sun blasted the room with warm brightness, and I woke up suddenly. I could hear Thor running around in the living room and talking to Mother. I rubbed my eyes and felt little beads of perspiration beginning to stand out on my forehead. I lay there a few minutes more and just listened to a switch engine at work in the yards.

The switchmen were making up trains, and the switch engine was kicking cars down different tracks. The whining sounds of the big diesel would alternately rise and fall. I would hear the squeaking of steel slowly turning on steel, and then after a long moment would come the great loud thud of a freight car banging in to couple up with a string of cars.

I finally got up and stretched. That part of my mind that did things without having to be told went about the business of getting me dressed. When I reached into my top dresser drawer to get a clean pair of socks, my hand touched something metallic. I picked up the wristwatch my parents had given me for Christmas. I was a little surprised to find my wristwatch where I had left it. I hadn't thought about the thing since the lilac day.

3

Dunnigan, Sanchez, and I were eating our lunches out behind the gym. We were about fifty yards up the mountainside and in amongst a stand of cedar trees. Some boulders cropped out there and were just right for lounging on. The setting was peaceful and lilac bushes were in bloom all around us. We kept the spot our own little secret, and we would sneak up there to eat lunch and to stay out of the way of troublesome upperclassmen.

Sanchez asked me what time it was. I reached in my pocket and pulled out my wristwatch. Dunnigan, who was wearing his fancy wristwatch, already knew the time.

"It's twenty-two minutes to one, Pancho."

I looked at my wristwatch and said, "That's about right."

"I'm exactly right," Dunnigan added. "I checked it with my father's railroad watch this morning."

"Well, I'll be darned if I care." I shoved my wristwatch back in my pocket.

"Did you break your watch strap or something?" Sanchez asked.

"No, I just don't like to wear the stupid thing."

"You should get yourself an expandable band." Dunnigan pulled at his wristwatch and showed me how well the fancy stretch band worked. "It's snug, but it moves with your wrist, and you hardly know you're wearing a watch."

"No, that wouldn't do any good," I said. I didn't like feeling the strap on my wrist, but that wasn't all that bothered me. "I don't like wristwatches, because I don't believe in wearing wristwatches."

Sanchez, who didn't own a wristwatch, looked up suddenly. He had just taken a big bite out of a peanut butter sandwich, but that didn't stop him.

"I thought a wristwatch was fun to wear."

"No fun at all. Anyhow I don't believe in wristwatches," I said.

"You don't believe in wristwatches?" Dunnigan asked.

"As far as I'm concerned, wristwatches are a big waste of time."

"Hah!" Sanchez blurted with his mouth full of peanut butter sandwich. He and I both knew what was coming. I had shown great disrespect for fancy wristwatches, and Dunnigan was rising to the bait.

"Are you serious?"

"Sure, I'm serious."

"Then," Dunnigan paused and pointed a finger at the sky. "I shall question you in the manner of Socrates."

"Ha hah!" Sanchez laughed. He was always ready to listen to a good argument.

Ever since Dunnigan had read about a guy named Socrates, our arguments had turned into question-and-answer debates. Dunnigan's mother was a very intelligent lady. She had done a lot of reading, and she even knew all about the Russian Revolution. She had influenced Dunnigan to read great literature, and he had stumbled onto Socrates. Sanchez and I didn't know anything about Socrates, but we did love to argue.

"Do you believe that wristwatches are useful?" Dunnigan asked.

"Sure, they're useful for people who like to wear

them and who always want to know the minutes and hours."

"Would you say that wristwatches help people to keep track of time?"

"No, I wouldn't say that."

"Do you believe in time? Are you aware of the idea?"

"I believe I got a pretty good idea what time is."

"Then you do keep track of time, don't you?"

"Sure, but I don't need a wristwatch to keep track of time with."

"Then," Dunnigan paused and pointed his finger at me. "What time is it?"

"Ha hah!" Sanchez laughed again. "No fair reaching in your pocket, Collins."

"No problem," I said. "The time is the present. The time is today. It's not yesterday, it's not tomorrow, but it's right now."

"Aw, I knew that," Sanchez said.

"Doesn't everybody know we live in the present?" Dunnigan asked.

"Sure, and that's why the present is so easy to lose track of. Nobody thinks it's important."

"Wait a minute." Sanchez held up a hand. "How can you lose track of something that's always there?"

"You start by wearing a wristwatch, that's how.

Then you'll start worrying because you should have been somewhere ten minutes ago, or you'll start fretting because you have to kill twenty minutes before you can do something you want to. You'll worry and fret about the past or the future, and you'll end up by making a big mess out of the present."

"You really believe all that?" Sanchez asked.

"Am I telling you? Why do you think I keep my wristwatch in my pocket?"

"Don't you think that you could avoid all those problems if you made correct use of your wristwatch?" Dunnigan asked.

"All I know is I don't want clocks all the time telling me what to do."

"How are you going to know when to do things?" Dunnigan asked.

"The Indians really knew when to do things. They didn't have to worry about minutes and hours."

"I knew it," Sanchez said. "We always start out with Socrates and end up with the Indians."

"I'll tell you one thing," Dunnigan said. "We're not Indians." He paused and pointed to his watch." "In nine minutes the bell will ring, and we'll all have to show up in Spanish class."

"Yeah, old Mr. Garcia would sure miss us." Sanchez smiled at the prospect.

"Well, we have to go to school and be on time like everybody else," I said. "It's the law, but we don't have to believe it's the only way to learn what's important."

"This whole country runs on clocks and watches," Dunnigan said. "It'll be the same thing when we get out in life and have to go to work."

"I'd rather do something real interesting, so I wouldn't have to watch a clock."

"You'd still have to know what time it was."

"If I was real interested in something, I wouldn't care. I'd get there early and I'd stay late."

"He's right, Dunnigan," Sanchez said. "He's always the first one out to the track field and the last one to hit the showers."

"When I'm doing something important, I forget the time. That's how come I know what's important. I never learned anything important from a wristwatch."

"A wristwatch is only a convenience . . . ," Dunnigan started.

"Convenience? A guy could end up having a wristwatch for a brain. A guy could go through life always thinking twenty minutes ahead of himself. He could worry all he wanted to, but he would just end up dying and be twenty minutes short."

"When you get an idea, Collins, you do pound it into the ground, don't you?"

"Since I did all this talking, I made up my mind. I'll never wear a wristwatch again. I won't even carry it around in my pocket. That's my final word."

"I think if Socrates were here, he could talk you right out of it."

"Well, Socrates lived his life, and now I'm going to live mine."

"Hey, don't those lilac flowers smell good, though?" Sanchez asked.

"Yeah," I said.

"Let me show you something. Come here." Sanchez stepped over to the nearest lilac bush and grabbed two handfuls of lilac blossoms. He squashed the blossoms and rubbed his hands together. He put his hands up to his face and took a deep breath.

"Ha hah! Does that smell good!" Sanchez laughed. He grabbed more blossoms, squashed them in his hands, and then ran his fingers through his hair. Dunnigan and I watched him repeat the process. Finally Sanchez pulled out his comb and combed his hair. He gave us a sly smile.

"Try it," he said. "Lilac flowers is the greatest natural hair tonic known to man." Dunnigan and I looked at one another. I shrugged my shoulders.

"I'll give it a try if Pancho says so." I rubbed a lot of lilac blossoms between my hands and anointed my head with the juicy fragrance. Dunnigan had to go along with the experiment. As we combed our hair, Dunnigan glanced at his watch.

"The bell will ring in exactly two minutes. We better start back."

Dunnigan, Sanchez, and I made it to Spanish class on time that day, but we brought with us the heavy sweet fragrance of lilac blossoms. We took our customary seats near the back of the room, but before long the girls around us started to giggle as the fragrance of lilacs began to tease its way from desk to desk. Old Mr. Garcia, who was quick to anger at the least disturbance, knew something was amiss. He glared suspiciously at us, but we put on our best poker faces and played innocent.

"I don't know what ninnies are causing this disturbance," Mr. Garcia shouted, "but this has got to stop!"

Dunnigan, Sanchez, and I didn't move a muscle. We pretended to be perfect students. Old Mr. Garcia didn't know whom to blame. We thought it was great fun. Old Mr. Garcia knew we were up to something. He knew we were the troublemakers, but he couldn't prove it. He didn't have the nose for it.

That night before I went to bed, I remembered about my wristwatch. I slipped it under some socks in the top drawer of my dresser. I figured that sooner or later Thor would be digging around in there. Thor would like my wristwatch. He would know how to have a lot of fun with it. I knew that when Thor got through playing with my wristwatch, the stupid thing wouldn't be keeping track of any more minutes and hours.

4

I looked at my wristwatch once more and wondered why Thor hadn't found it. He had a talent for getting into things. I dropped the watch back in the drawer, picked out a clean pair of socks, and finished getting dressed.

After I got out of the bathroom, Thor came running up to tell me that last night he had fallen out of bed and had slept all night on the floor. I told him I didn't believe it.

I went into the kitchen and told Mother I didn't want any cereal. We had some bananas, so I ate two bananas and drank some milk. I sat in the kitchen for a while, and Mother finally persuaded me to take out the garbage. On the way I stopped to feed and water the pigeons. When I got back to the kitchen, I decided to have another glass of milk.

Mother had watered the garden early in the morning. She remarked on how well the carrots and radishes were doing and complimented me for having done such a good job putting in the garden. I said I had enjoyed working on it. Turning the ground over had been tough, but the planting had been easy. Mother said the weeds were getting thick between the rows of carrots and radishes. She thought I would have time to hoe some weeds before going swimming.

I started to grumble, but Mother reminded me that the garden had been as much my idea as hers. She said I should hoe just one row of weeds. Then I might see if I could hoe another. I sipped at my glass of milk and thought how well I knew what Mother was up to.

When I was five years old, I had a milk glass with a lot of different colored rings around it. Sometimes in the morning I wouldn't want to drink my milk, but Mother would have much to say about that.

"Now, Leif, drink this nice fresh milk. It's good for you."

I would shake my head.

"Look, Leif. See the yellow line? It's not very far to the yellow line. You could drink down to the yellow line."

I would look at the milk level and at the yellow line, and I would take a sip.

"See, you went right to the top of the yellow line. That was very good, except you can just see a little bit of milk above the yellow line. Take one more sip, and you'll be at the bottom of the yellow line."

By this time I would probably take a good drink of milk, and Mother would act surprised.

"My goodness, you went right past the purple line altogether. Why, you're almost to the red line!"

She would keep me going past the red line, past the gold line, and right to the bottom of the glass. Mother could take a glass of milk and split it up into a dozen little parts. Somehow she would get me interested in seeing that glass of milk the same way she saw it, and that was how she got me to drink a lot of milk.

I looked out at the garden which stretched along the far side of our property. I could see how hot it was out there. Mother took a load of dirty clothes out to the washer and dryer on the back porch. She warned me that I would have to get busy if I planned to go swimming early.

I drained the last of the milk from the glass and got up slowly. I pushed myself out the door and down the front steps. Thor followed me out to the garden. He kept telling me that I had to hoe those weeds. The hoe had been lying in the sun and was too hot to hold. I got the garden hose and ran cold water over the handle. Then I threw off my T-shirt and went to work.

Thor kept teasing me about having to hoe the weeds, but I tried to ignore him. At last I told him to shut up, but I knew it wouldn't do any good. I put my head down and chopped weeds at a steady pace. Finally Thor went over to swing on the climbing rope that hung down from a big limb of the oak tree that stood in the front yard between the garden and the house.

My arms and shoulders glistened with sweat, and sweat dripped off my forehead. I felt drops of sweat running down my back. The dirt was getting dry in the hot sun, and dust swirled up to tickle my nose, but I didn't let up. I worked a long time before Thor came over to taunt me again.

This time I threw down the hoe and made straight for the garden hose. Thor knew what was coming. I grabbed the hose nozzle and turned the water on full blast. Thor started to run, but he fell down. He had trouble getting up, because I hit him with a heavy stream of water and soaked him from head to foot.

Thor struggled to his feet, and he was as mad as a wet cat. He shook his little fist at me as I continued to douse him good. He was shouting at me and telling me that I was no fair. I thought he might start crying, so I let up and turned off the water.

Then Thor started to cry and yell for Mother. He clambered up the front steps and onto the porch. Mother had come to the front door. She gave a startled cry and locked the screen door to keep Thor out. He really started to cry his eyes out, but Mother hushed him quickly. She told him to take off his wet clothes right there on the front porch, and she would get a towel to dry him off. Thor sputtered a bit but started to undress. I went back to my hoeing.

I was working down along the last row of radishes when I heard someone start to turn on the garden hose. I whirled around and roared like a cougar. I threw the hoe in the air and charged straight at Thor who had his swim trunks on and was getting ready to squirt me with the hose. He could have gotten me easily, but he hesitated and I roared at him again.

Thor dropped the hose and started to run across the yard. He was yelling for Mother, but then he noticed that Mother was standing on the front porch and she was watching us. Thor stopped.

Mother told us that this was about enough. She told me to set up the sprinkler on the lawn so that Thor could play in the water. I had done enough garden work for one day, and she had made a pitcher of lemonade. She told me to come in and cool off, and she wanted to talk to me.

I got the water going on the front lawn, and Thor started his ritualistic dance around the sprinkler. He giggled as he ran in and out and jumped around trying to avoid the spray.

I put my T-shirt back on and went up to the kitchen where a tall glass of lemonade was waiting for me on the kitchen table. I sat down and rubbed my hands over my face to get rid of some of the grimy sweat. I wiped my hands on my T-shirt. Mother sat down to join me. She thought I had worked hard. I sipped some lemonade and said I had gotten most of the weeds. Mother said she was pleased to see that I could always do a good job when I put my mind to it.

Then she told me that she wished I wouldn't be so rough with Thor. I grumbled and told Mother why I had sprayed Thor. She understood all that. She just wanted me to be more careful. She considered how easily the powerful spray from the hose nozzle could have hit Thor in the eye and caused an injury; and since Thor was sopping wet as he stumbled up the front steps, he could have easily slipped and hurt himself.

I said I hadn't meant for anything like that to happen. Mother was sure I hadn't meant any harm, but I was old enough and intelligent enough to know how easily accidents could happen. Thor was barely four years old; he still needed a lot of protecting.

Mother told me that I had a responsibility to see that Thor didn't have any needless accidents. She told me to think about it and not let Thor bother me so much.

After all Thor trusted me and looked up to me. If he did pester me, he just wanted some attention from his big brother. I said I understood and I would be more careful from now on. Mother suggested that I might even spend more time playing with Thor, but I started to grumble again.

I finished my lemonade and said I would go swimming. Mother wanted me to have another lemonade and talk some more with her, but I had done my work and was set on going early. She thought I should at least get cleaned up before I went, but I said it didn't matter anyhow, because the lifeguard always made us take a shower before he let us in the pool.

I went out to the back porch, got my swim trunks, and rolled them up in a towel. Mother resigned herself to my leaving. She saw me to the door. She told me to have a good day, and she told me to be careful walking along the highway.

I said I would keep my eyes open and be very careful. I didn't want Mother thinking I might get hit by a car. The fewer worries Mother had concerning me, the better off I was. I had learned that from experience.

I went down the front stairs two at a time, strode across the catwalk, and bounded up the cement steps to the highway. Thor was still playing in the sprinkler, but he stopped to watch me leave. I took a deep breath of freedom and started off along the shoulder of the highway.

I had gone about a dozen paces when I turned to glance back. Thor was still standing there, and he was still watching me. Then I stopped and waved good-bye, and Thor waved back.

5

I picked up my heels and jogged a ways just to loosen up my body. I felt great. I listened to the sound of my gym shoes crunching in the gravel and imagined that I was chewing up the road. I felt as if I could run forever, but I slowed to a walk. I looked up the highway and watched the heat waves dancing on the black asphalt. The swimming pool was on the other side of town and a good two miles from home, so I had to take it easy.

I decided to do the Scout's Pace and alternate walking and jogging until I got to the concrete. I walked fifty paces and jogged fifty paces. As I walked, I felt the sweat oozing on my skin. My T-shirt was soaked and sticking to my chest, but the jogging caused a slight breeze that felt cool.

I happened to be jogging as I went by Manfreidi's Quick Stop. I saw that Manfreidi, who was a good friend to Father, was out front pumping some gas. Manfreidi turned as he heard me crunching by. He straightened up suddenly.

"Hey, Leif! You a dumb kid or something?" He wiped a gob of sweat off his forehead. "You want to get sunstroke?"

"Well, I'm going swimming."

"Wait'll I tell the big Irishman I see his dumb kid running down the highway and it is ninety-nine degrees in the shade!"

I lost track of my jogging, so I just jogged a ways farther before I slowed to a walk. The air was still and the heat seemed to close in on me. It was like walking in an oven. I counted fifty steps and started to jog again, but I was beginning to worry about sunstroke. I remembered reading something about it in a first aid manual. I jogged past Diamond Match Lumber and decided to stop in some shade near the city limits sign.

A creek came coursing down the mountainside

there. The cold splashing water gurgled into an iron pipe under the highway and spewed out on rocks below the embankment. A current of cool air flowed down along with the creek toward the river. I stopped in some shade and felt the cool breeze drifting across the highway.

The moist air was freshly scented by damp fir and pine and by mountain mint and wild lilac. My nose reminded me there was a dogwood tree not far up the draw. I took a couple of deep breaths and my whole body seemed to snap right back together again.

A big diesel truck and semitrailer roared by, and a blast of hot dusty air buffeted me. I considered that a guy should be able to take care of himself, and knowing about something like sunstroke he shouldn't take any needless chances. One fact stuck in my mind. I sure didn't want to come down with a case of sunstroke right after Manfreidi hollered at me about it.

Near the city limits sign a crude footpath angled down the hillside and roughly followed the creek to the railroad tracks where the path ended and where the creek flowed into a huge cement drain beneath the roadbed. The path existed mainly by virtue of some railroad men who lived farther up the mountainside and who came down this way to go to work. In my travels I sometimes used the path on the way to fishing or on the way to Dunnigan's house. Dunnigan lived across the river which ran down along the far side of the freight yards.

Whether I was going fishing or to visit Dunnigan, I had to cut across the freight yards, and that was another concern I didn't want Mother thinking about. Making a mistake crossing the freight yards could be worse than getting sunstroke, that was for sure.

I recalled what happened to me once earlier that summer when I was in a rush to get to Dunnigan's house. I hot-footed it down this same path but had to pull up short at the tracks. My way was blocked by a very slow-moving freight train.

The boxcars moaned and creaked as they inched by, and I could see I was in for a long wait. I considered climbing up the side of a boxcar, across the top, and down the other side, but I didn't like the idea of crawling across the top of a moving boxcar. Then an empty flatcar came creeping along, and I started to get impatient again. I could climb onto the flatcar, walk across, and simply jump off the other side.

I jogged over to the end of the flatcar, grabbed the handrail with both hands, and kicked my left foot up to the step bar. Just as I put my weight on my left foot, it slipped. In that instant my body started to swing in under the flatcar. All my feeling was in my left foot. I knew it was dangling close to a pair of monstrous grinding wheels.

I pushed back with my hands, let go of the handrail, and lit flat on my back in the gravel. It might have been a feather bed for all I knew. I jerked back my left leg and was greatly relieved to find that my foot was still on the end of it. I scrambled up and stepped back to wait.

I wiggled the toes on my left foot. I felt the threads of the sock I was wearing; I felt the worn spots in the inner sole of my gym shoe, and I felt the sharp pointed rocks in the gravel I was standing on. I felt lucky and I felt stupid.

I hadn't stopped to think. I hadn't used my head. I wasn't afraid of freight trains or yard engines or boxcars or flatcars, I wasn't afraid to cut across the rows of steel track, but I was afraid of being stupid. I had been taught better than that.

6

When Father took me down the path behind our old house to go fishing for the first time, he stopped a few steps up the embankment from the freight yards and spent a moment looking in one direction and then in the other. He studied the whole yards. Then he looked down at me, but he didn't say anything.

I was ten. Earlier that year Father had found work as a brakeman on the Southern Pacific Railroad, and we had come to Dunsmuir. The small railroad town lay strung out down a wide canyon, and a few miles to the north mighty Mt. Shasta raised its year-round whitecap fourteen thousand feet in the sky. The mountains of northern California were quite a change from the plains of North Dakota. For a time I imagined we were living in a picture postcard, but the river seemed real enough to me.

For as long as I could remember I had wanted to

be a fisherman, and here the Sacramento River was a cold clear trout stream. Father didn't know much about trout fishing, but Mother had been after him for weeks to get me started. He had bought me a metal telescope pole, a reel, some line, leader, hooks, split shot sinkers, and a jar of salmon eggs. Finally Mother talked him into taking me down to the river. To get there we had to cross the freight yards.

I asked Father if we weren't going fishing. He nodded and we started down to cross the tracks. He pointed at the first set of rails and said it was the main line. A freight or passenger train could come by fast from either direction, and a speeding engine could squash a railroad man as easily as a bug is squashed against a car windshield. Just standing too close to the main line could be a mistake, and a railroad man usually only got to make one mistake.

He recalled a young brakeman who had been walking too close to the main line. A passenger train had come by fast, and something protruding from the engine, probably a handrail, struck the brakeman in the head, crushing his skull and killing him instantly. I wondered why the brakeman hadn't heard the train coming.

Father said that sometimes railroad sounds did strange things. A fast-moving engine could come right on top of its own noise. Here in the freight yards the echoing of sounds could be misleading.

25

Snow was dangerous. In the snow freight cars could move quietly. Father told me that early in the year he had almost been run over by a flatcar in the snow. He jumped aside just in time, and the flatcar had gone by him without a sound. He said that a railroad man had to trust his eyes and not his ears. As we crossed the yards, we kept looking in both directions to see that the tracks were clear.

I considered that Father had a dangerous job, and he admitted the fact. A railroad man had no business forgetting his job was dangerous. That was why safety was the number one rule in the book.

We went around a short string of boxcars, and Father said he always went at least a car-length beyond the last car before he cut across the tracks. Any standing freight car was liable to move suddenly without warning. If the yard crew kicked a heavy boxcar hard into a string of cars that wasn't tied down well, the whole string could easily be jolted another car-length down the track.

Our way was blocked again by a long string of cars; and as we walked along beside it, Father mentioned that a railroad man would never try to take a short cut across the yards by climbing under a boxcar or between boxcars.

He pointed to a pair of large steel wheels and asked me to think about how heavy they were. Boxcars weighed tons, and even their wheels weighed thousands of pounds. Those wheels didn't just run over people, they ran right through them. The wheels didn't have to be going fast to cut off an arm or a leg, because the crushing weight did the cutting.

He pointed to the huge couplings between boxcars and said that when a kicked car hit into a string of cars, those couplings slammed together with enough force to completely crush the hand or the arm that got mixed up between them.

Father said a railroad man had a lot to watch out for in the freight yards. Sometimes one look wasn't enough. At a glance a railroad man could notice an engine or boxcar coming down the track, but he might not see an empty flatcar if he didn't take a second look. Empty flatcars had caused a lot of grief.

We finally skirted the long string of cars and watchfully crossed rows of empty tracks to where a path led down to the river. Father started to tell me what he had learned about trout fishing by talking to a fellow brakeman.

At the river he rigged the pole and showed me how to make a leader. He cut a length of nylon leader material, knotted a loop in one end, and tied a hook on the other. With a stone he tapped one of the split shot sinkers on the leader several inches above the hook. He said the transparent nylon would be almost invisible in the water. The trout were smart, and they wouldn't bite if they saw the line.

He looped the leader to the fishing line and baited the hook. He said the salmon egg had to completely hide the hook and the egg had to move with the current of the river; otherwise, the trout wouldn't be fooled.

Father said that trout usually hung around behind big rocks and stayed out of the fast water. He said he would make a few casts and show me how to swing the bait out and gently drop it into the water. He tried to cast the line out just above a big rock so that the egg would float down into the calmer water.

He made several casts. Finally I said I was ready to try, but he told me to wait. I told him I was the one who was supposed to do the fishing. He laughed and said I had all summer to catch trout, but right now he wanted to try. I resigned myself to waiting, but after a few more casts he reeled in the line a little and handed me the pole.

Father told me to get home before dark, and he started to leave. I asked him how he could go home when he was supposed to be teaching me how to fish. He said that right now I knew just as much about trout fishing as he did. Catching trout wasn't going to be as easy as it sounded, and I was going to have to learn by experience. He wished me good luck and went up the path.

Suddenly I was alone.

7

Another diesel truck roared by and left me standing in a cloud of dust. I spit some dust out of my mouth and wiped my eyes. I needed to get a drink of water, and I needed a good cooling-off, so I wouldn't be worrying about sunstroke anymore.

I went a few yards down the footpath and cut into the underbrush between me and the creek. I pushed by some limbs and came out just below where the creek cascaded out of the iron pipe and splashed onto a jumble of large black rocks. I found a tiny pool and got down on my hands and knees to take a drink. The water was ice cold. I washed my face and splashed water all over my head and on the back of my neck.

I suddenly felt cold. My brain seemed to tighten up inside my head. I noticed how the little twigs and pebbles in the pool were magnified by the cold clear water. The steady sound of rushing water broke in on some strange silence. I felt a tingling between my shoulder blades, and I shivered as I got to my feet.

The waters gurgled and sang. Cool air drifted over me. I felt the hair rising on the back of my neck and knew this was a magic place. The feeling took me back. I was alone again with the fishing pole in my hand and a river swirling past me.

The trees along the river waved their boughs and fluttered their leaves to look at me. Glistening blades of grass squirmed beneath my feet. The whole riverbank knew I was there. Even the stones listened as the river murmured things about me, but I couldn't quite make out the words.

I made several nervous casts before my hands stopped shaking. I didn't move far along the river that day, but I did try different spots. I got snagged a lot and broke some leaders. Making new ones took time.

I was looking for another spot when I noticed that the line of sunlight had climbed halfway up the east side of the canyon. The day was almost over, and I hadn't even gotten a bite. I packed up my gear and started for home. The river would be here again tomorrow, and I knew I was a fisherman.

At dusk I clumped up the front stairs, and Father met me at the door.

"Did you catch a trout?"

"Not yet . . . but I was real careful crossing the yards."

"Hush about that," he said, and we went into the kitchen where Mother served me some hot dogs and beans. She had even baked me a potato. I felt hungry all over.

"Well, Leif, did you enjoy fishing?" she asked.

"Yes, I will make a great trout fisherman."

"That's nice . . . I hope you were careful crossing the tracks."

"Yes, Mother." I glanced at Father, but he just looked up at the ceiling a little bit.

8

I dreamed of a highway just above me where the black asphalt was getting soft in the hot sun.

I turned and my knees trembled as I bent low to push through the underbrush. In my wanderings I had found many magic places, but I had never gotten used to the uneasy feeling that came over me when I saw a place in a strange new way. I scrambled up to the city limits sign and popped out into the warm brightness.

I started jogging along past the cemetery. When I got to where the cement sidewalk started, I was sweating again. I slowed to a walk and noticed some wavy lines in the cement. At this very spot I met Sanchez for the first time.

We studied each other as we passed. Out of the corner of my eye I saw him stop and turn. I did likewise as he hailed me.

"Hey, you a new kid in town?"

"Yeah."

"I could tell. I see you walking around town like you are getting the feel of the place."

"Yeah."

"What grade you in?"

"I'll be in the sixth grade."

"Hey, me too. I'll be in the sixth grade."

"No kidding. What's your name?"

"My name's Francisco Sanchez, but my friends call me 'Pancho.' "

"My name's Leif Collins."

"Leif? What kind of name is that?"

"It's a Viking name. My mother's folks came from Norway."

"Oh, yeah? Well, I'll call you 'Collins.' "

"Okay, Pancho."

"Hah! So you want to fight?"

"What?"

"You know. You're a new kid in town . . . so you want to fight?"

"No . . . I mean I'd like to, but I can't. I promised my mother I wouldn't fight."

"Oh."

"My father was a fighter. He even did some semi-pro. My mother didn't like that."

"I guess not," Sanchez said.

"Anyway, my father says fighting's no percentage. He says nobody wins a fight."

"Well, I guess it's not really necessary."

"I better be getting along. I suppose I'll see you when school starts."

"Hah! I'm looking for a long summer. Say, don't you do any swimming?"

"Well, I can do some."

"Pretty soon will be swimming season. You can come down to Blackberry Hole. That's at the end of Butterfly Avenue across the tracks."

"Yeah, I'd like to do some swimming, but I'd have

to ask my folks."

"Sure. Maybe I'll see you down there this summer."

"Yeah, I'll see you later."

"Good-bye," Sanchez said, and we parted.

I took a few steps before I turned to watch Sanchez continue on his way. I noticed the swagger in his stride. He seemed big for a sixth-grader. I was nearly as tall as he was, but he was very stocky. I was glad he was reasonable about me not being able to fight.

Of course we did become friends. That fall when we started school, Sanchez didn't make any secret of the fact that I was a friend of his. I never did have any trouble with the bigger kids, not even with those in the next grade up. Sanchez was easygoing and seemed to have a natural respect for everyone. I wouldn't have expected him to fight any battles for me, but somehow I never did get picked on.

Then just before my fourteenth summer I started to grow out of my clothes. Father was six feet tall, and I was fast approaching him. I worked hard to make the basketball team, and I had a great season running track. I filled out some and began to be respected as an athlete. Almost overnight I found myself three inches taller and just as strong as Sanchez. He looked up at me now, and he seemed proud that we were friends. I came to realize how much I appreciated him. Sanchez had taught me something about friendship.

By the time I got through thinking about Sanchez, I was at another remembering spot, the corner where I met Dunnigan for the first time; and that happened right after I caught my first trout.

9

After Father got me started fishing that first summer, I went day after day without catching a trout. I fished behind every rock I could reach and gradually worked my way upstream and through town. I tried Blackberry Hole and behind the roundhouse and spent several days trying a couple of pools above the roundhouse. I followed the river up as far as the Bend which was a deep hole just downstream from where the cement highway bridge arched high across the river north of town.

Late one afternoon I finished another uneventful day of fishing at the first broad pool above the roundhouse. I undid the leader, reeled in the line, and telescoped the metal pole. I didn't feel much like a fisherman, but I knew that the trout were there and that someday I would learn to catch them. As I turned to start home, I saw a man coming down toward me. He was carrying a basket creel and a long cardboard tube.

"Hi, any luck?" he asked.

"No, not today."

"Well, let's see what I can do." He set the creel on a flat rock.

He uncapped the cardboard tube and from a cloth lining withdrew the three sections of a bamboo fly rod. Deftly but carefully he assembled the rod and gave it a flick for good measure. He put on a reel and threaded the line. He handed me the rod and asked me to hold it.

It was as light as a feather compared to my telescope pole. The weight of the reel gave the rod perfect balance. The shafts of split bamboo had a shiny coat of varnish, but I could see the rod wasn't new. The cork handle was very worn.

The man reached in his creel and fished out a long leader which he looped to the end of the line. I noticed an extra loop in the leader and asked him about it.

"This leader's for fly fishing," he said. "I use two flies."

He opened a small white box and studied a moment before picking out two flies. He noticed I was leaning over to get a look at the flies, so he held them up for me to see.

"This is a gray hackle-red . . . and this is a gray hackle-yellow."

He looped the flies on the leader and said he was ready. I handed him the rod. He stepped onto a large rock and took another moment to study the river.

The man seemed to be a bit younger than Father, but I could tell he was a railroad man. The lines in his face were etched with soot and grime. He must have just gotten off work.

He told me to keep to the side, and he started to flick the rod back and forth as he let the line out to make a cast. He let more and more line out until it was swirling back and forth in a long figure-eight pattern. He seemed to be taking a measurement. Then as the line rolled out above the water, he raised the rod slightly and let the flies whip out to the end of the line and start down. They dropped gently to the surface of the water near a riffle at the head of the pool.

I watched the flies float slowly into the current of deep water. Most of the line was still off the water.

Not more than two seconds went by before it happened. A small burst of water erupted over one of the flies.

The man flicked the rod straight up, and the line went taut. The rod bent and the tip started a furious dance. I couldn't see the trout, but the line zigzagged toward us and downstream as the man played the trout into the calmer water on the near side. Then I saw the trout flash as it darted back and forth against the pull of the line. Finally the trout broke water, and the man reeled it into a shallow spot amongst the rocks. I got down and watched the man pick up the trout by hooking a forefinger under its gills.

"What a beauty!" I said.

"Fair size trout." He unhooked the fly.

"Sure is a big one."

"Well, just good eating size." He popped the trout into his creel.

I wanted a chance to look at the trout some more, but the man stepped onto the large rock again, and I had to get out of the way. He started to cast again, and I felt as if I were about to see a movie the second time through. I knew what was going to happen and it did. He landed another fair size trout.

"Another beauty! I knew there must be trout in here!"

"Don't let anybody tell you any different. There are plenty of trout in this river."

"I sure hope so."

"Time for a few more." He put the trout in his creel.

"I've got to get going. I have to be home before dark."

"Well, good luck with your fishing. I was about your age when I got started."

"No kidding?"

"Sure, you'll do fine."

"Thanks." I started up the embankment.

"Hey!" he called after me. "You be careful up there. Keep your eyes open!"

"Don't worry," I called back. "My father's a brakeman."

"Good!" he said, and he waved good-bye.

I got home in time for a half-warm supper and a mild discussion with Mother about the meaning of the words "home before dark."

I cleaned up my plate and was telling Mother about fly fishing when I suddenly looked up and saw Father standing in the kitchen doorway. He was just home from work. I saw that he had tilted back his railroad cap, because his face was black with soot below the line across his forehead. His lantern was hooked over his arm, and he was leaning against the doorjamb as if he had been there for some time.

Mother looked up from doing dishes and was startled. She asked Father why he always had to appear like an apparition instead of coming into the house like a normal person.

Father laughed. He gave Mother a kiss and a pat. He told her he would drink a cup of coffee before his bath, and by then she would be finished with the dishes and be able to scrub his back. Mother handed him a cup. He sat down at the kitchen table.

"Well, you catch a trout yet?" he asked.

"Not yet," I said. "I need a gray hackle-red and a gray hackle-yellow."

"What's that?"

"Fishing flies . . . one's called a gray hackle-red and another one's called a gray hackle-yellow."

"Oh. . . ." He drank some coffee.

10

Father never did say anything about the fishing flies, but I got up one morning a few days later and found two fishing flies on the kitchen table.

"Oh boy!" I said. "A gray hackle-red and a gray hackle-yellow. Just what I wanted!"

Mother started to laugh. She said she would never understand how I could get so excited over such little things. I started to explain that now I could do some fly fishing, but Mother said breakfast came first.

All I could think about was the fishing spot just above the roundhouse. I was eating breakfast so fast that Mother must have gotten nervous. She finally said I better go fishing. I grabbed my pole and the fishing flies and said I was on my way. Mother wished me luck.

I headed out the front door and started remembering how the young railroad man fished for trout. In my mind I saw how he cast the flies, and I imagined myself doing the same thing. I had a mile to walk, but my anticipation was great company.

As I cut across the tracks above the roundhouse, I saw the broad pool. My anticipation took another jump as I saw that no one else was there. I skidded down the embankment to the jumble of rocks near the water and stopped to set up my pole. My hands were quivering, and I had to settle down to make a leader with three loops. Finally I was ready.

I stepped onto the same large rock the railroad

man had stood on to make his casts. First, I studied the river. Then I let out some line and started to whip my pole back and forth. The telescope pole wobbled and creaked and caused me a lot of trouble. I managed to let out more line and try a cast, but the line and flies all plopped down in the shallows in front of me.

I tried again and again but couldn't do much better. I got down to the edge of the water and tried, and I even waded out to a rock I could stand on. I thought I made some good casts, but the line would always drop into a fast current, and the flies would be jerked along with it. I moved upstream to try behind some rocks, but nothing happened.

I was arm weary and feeling hungry, but I wasn't going to quit. Then I noticed the line of sunlight on the mountain. The day was just about gone. I reeled in, telescoped my pole, and headed for home. For company I had the anticipation of satisfying my hunger.

I was so pleased to get home to supper that Mother thought I must have caught a trout. She was sorry I hadn't and somewhat surprised that I wasn't getting discouraged.

My first day of fly fishing set a pattern that lasted for many days. Each morning after breakfast I picked up my pole and walked to the roundhouse. I tried there first and then went up or down the river looking for places. I whipped those flies back and forth until they were losing their hackles and bits of floss were starting to unravel. As far as I could see I hadn't even come close to catching a trout.

Then one afternoon I came back to the round-house and decided to try the lower end of the pool. I climbed down some rocks and made a couple casts but soon gave up. The water ran smooth and clear over the stony bottom, and I couldn't see any trout.

I thought to move a little upstream and didn't bother to reel in the line. I held out my pole as I started to climb over some rocks. A sudden pull upset my balance, and I jerked my pole straight up to catch myself. I looked back and saw a trout splashing furiously on the surface.

I struggled to hold the pole high and hauled in line as I scrambled down to the water. The trout splashed into a shallow spot between two rocks and gulped just long enough for me to hook a finger through its gills.

I picked up the trout and hurried to climb back up the rocks, but it started to whip its tail and wiggle off my finger. I threw down my pole and grabbed the trout with both hands. Then I got tangled in the line and fell down, but I didn't drop the fish. I stumbled halfway up the embankment and stopped to catch my breath. I could feel my heart beating in my throat, and I had to swallow a couple times.

The trout squirmed in my grasp and I felt how cold and slippery it was. I finally got a firm grip through its gills, so I could take a good look. The afternoon sun was still bright, and the flash of speckled rainbow colors dazzled my eyes. The trout squirmed in the sunlight and sparkled like a handful of precious gems. I was amazed. A pirate treasure worth a king's ransom would have looked the same.

The trout started flip-flopping again, so I knocked its head against a rock to stop its suffering. I got my gear together and cut a piece of line to loop through the trout's gills.

I was sure a lot of people saw me trudging homeward that afternoon, but no one seemed to take much notice of my trout on a string. Of course they couldn't have known I had just caught my first trout. Then I got to the corner a block from the cemetery, and someone yelled.

"Hey! Wait up!" I stopped and turned as a blond kid came running up. "You caught one. You caught a trout!"

"Yeah."

"I see you down by the river all the time, but you never catch any fish."

"Well, I've been trying."

"I knew you could do it. I knew you were a fisher-man."

"Thanks."

"Anyhow, you sure caught a big trout this time."

"Well, just good eating size."

Then we said good-bye, and later I learned his name was Dunnigan.

11

Sometimes on the long walk to the city swimming pool I would do some jogging and think about how great a long distance runner I was going to be, and I would plan out strategies for winning the three-quarter mile. Sometimes I would think about making the basketball team, and sometimes I would think about hiking, mountain climbing, or camping out.

Sometimes I would think about growing up, but that was a sad thing for me to think about. I felt sorry for grown-up people, because they missed out on so many of the important things in life. Sometimes I would think about girls. I was interested all right, but I couldn't see how I would ever learn about girls until I grew up, and I wasn't in that big a hurry to grow up.

Sometimes I would notice remembering spots, and my mind would entertain me with scenes of my past experiences, but I had no way of knowing how my thoughts would wander amongst the bits and pieces of my memories. My mind was like a kaleidoscope. At the turn of a thought I would be startled by a brightly colored pattern all different than the last. Sometimes I would find myself halfway across town and not remember how I got there.

I continued up the next block. I was hot and sweaty but I felt strong inside. My legs were ready to stretch and run. I skipped across the next intersection but decided not to jog. Coach had told us not to do much running on cement sidewalks, because that kind of pounding could take the spring out of our legs. The city swimming pool was still a long way off, but I was content to walk. My mind was good company, and the remembering spots were windows into the past. My mind was still busy thinking about my first summer in Dunsmuir.

12

By accident I caught a few more trout that summer, but none were as big as the one Dunnigan saw. I ran into Sanchez again several times and talked to him for a while at Manfreidi's where Mother had sent me for some groceries.

Early one afternoon Sanchez and a friend of his named Joey came to see me. They asked Mother if they could take me swimming down to Blackberry Hole. Mother was concerned about me learning to swim in the river. I reminded her that I already knew the dog paddle. Sanchez said the lower end of Blackberry Hole was shallow, and a guy could get in a lot of good practice. Joey said all the kids learned to swim there and a lot of grown-ups were always around.

I could see that Mother was resigned to letting me go. She wondered where I would be able to change into my swim trunks. Sanchez said they just wore their trunks under their clothes and never needed to worry about changing. Mother laughed, and I raced into my bedroom to get into my swim trunks. I got my clothes back on in a hurry, before Mother had a chance to change her mind. She made me promise to stay in the shallow end, and then she let me go. Sanchez told her that he would look out for me.

I heard the sounds of shouting and splashing as we came up the road to Blackberry Hole. A lot of kids were swimming and jumping around in the water. Some people were lounging on the rocks, and some were stretched out on towels.

Most of the big kids were upstream at the first deep pool. They were sitting on the Wall which was an eight-foot high, stone and concrete, retaining wall that followed the sharp bend of the river and kept the rushing water from washing out the road.

We stopped by a large tree near the calm shallow water of the lower pool.

"Good a place as any to leave our clothes," Sanchez said.

"Sure is a lot of people," I said.

"Yeah, it's swimming season, all right," Joey said.

"Hey, fisherman!" someone yelled. I turned and saw the blond kid climbing out of the water.

"Hi," I said.

"Hey, Dunnigan, do you know Collins?" Sanchez asked.

"Sure, Pancho, you should have seen the big trout this guy caught," Dunnigan said.

"When was this?" Sanchez looked at me.

"Quite a while ago. I ate it for supper the same night."

"Did you catch any more?" Dunnigan asked.

"A few . . . but I figure I got to work some on my swimming."

"Yeah, the water's great!" Dunnigan said.

He scampered back into the water, took a couple of running steps, and jumped out flat on his belly. He made a big splash. Sanchez and I started to inch our way into the water. It felt cold at first.

"The best way to get used to the water is to jump in all at once," Joey said.

He climbed onto one of the rocks that jutted out into the river and jumped. His splash helped get us wet. Then Dunnigan came up splashing us, and we couldn't do anything about it, except splash back. Finally I ducked my head under the water a few times and I was used to it. I got down to work on my dog paddle. I felt strong.

"You swim pretty good," Sanchez said.

"I need a lot of practice, because I want to learn the overhand crawl stroke."

Father had been a good swimmer. I had talked to

him about learning the overhand crawl stroke, and I had watched a lot of it on the Saturday afternoon reruns of old Tarzan movies. I clasped my hands together, pushed out flat on my face, and did the steamboat kick. Then I started the overhand stroke, but my kick fell apart, and I ended up hacking the water with my arms. I blew bubbles and turned my head to grab a breath of air, but I got a mouthful of water and jumped up gagging.

"You can't expect to get it all at once," Sanchez said.

"I will get it. I will get it all at once, or I will swallow this whole river trying."

I kept practicing. Sometimes I managed to pop my head out of the water and get a good breath of air, so I could keep on jerking my legs and chopping my arms through the water. I put up a fierce struggle and fought until I made some headway against the slow moving current. Sanchez and Dunnigan did some practicing with me. I could see they had almost as much trouble with the overhand crawl stroke as I did.

A high jumble of boulders cropped up where the Wall ended down alongside the lower pool. We sat around on the rocks there to dry off and rest, but soon we got hot and had to jump back in the river. We spent the rest of the afternoon jumping and diving off the lower boulders. I did a lot of bellyflops until I learned to bend at the waist as I dove out and to duck my head between my arms as I hit the water.

"How was that one?" I looked at Sanchez.

"Your legs flop over a lot." Sanchez was always the one to give an honest appraisal, and I was left wondering why I had asked the question.

"At least it wasn't a bellyflop," I said at last.

I was happy to get home that night and tell Mother how great the river was for swimming. She seemed relieved and pleased that I had gotten in some good practice.

13

As the days went by, Mother got used to the routine of me going down to Blackberry Hole. I got over a slight sunburn and turned as brown as a roasted turkey. I kept practicing the overhand crawl stroke and started to feel good at it.

"I think I'll swim across the river."

"You'll end up down to the bridge," Dunnigan said.

"Aw, he might make it," Sanchez said.

"Well, I'll get myself a good start."

I waded upstream and stopped to get a good breath. Then I launched myself straight into the fast current. I hacked and chopped and kicked. I popped my head up for air and kept at it. The river swept me downstream, but I made it across in good shape just ahead of the rapids that took off from the bottom of Blackberry Hole. I walked upstream on the other side, plunged in, and fought my way back across to the outcropping of boulders.

"Way to go, Collins," Dunnigan said.

"Yeah, that's pretty good. You didn't swallow the whole river after all," Sanchez said.

"Well, let's do some diving."

We spent a lot of time jumping and diving off the boulders. We were still hard at it and having a lot of fun when a big kid came down and climbed to the top of the highest boulder which rose to a point well above our heads. We stopped to watch. The big kid swung his arms and dove straight out into the river. He made a shallow dive and hit the water with a loud splash.

"Man alive!" Dunnigan said.

"That's a pretty good dive," Sanchez said.

"I think I'll dive off that rock."

"You might not make it from there, Collins," Sanchez said. "You'd have to get out pretty far, or you'd hit bottom."

"That's almost as high as the Wall," Dunnigan said.

"Well, I'll give it a try."

Sanchez and Dunnigan watched as I climbed carefully to the top of the tall boulder. I planted my feet firmly and stood up to look the situation over. I saw the rocks and the shallow water below me. I studied how far out the deeper water was. I knew I had the spring in my legs to get there, but I would still have to make a shallow dive. I bent at the knees a few times to test my footing.

I hadn't thought that the boulder would seem so high. I was a little surprised at the difference between looking at the top of the boulder and climbing up to stand on it. Of course my eyes were about four feet higher than the top of the boulder now, and maybe that made the difference.

The boulder wasn't as high as the Wall, but I looked around and saw that I stood head and shoulders above the Wall. I glanced up to where the big kids were, and one of them was pointing at me and saying something to another big kid. Then Joey started to climb out onto a rock below me.

"Hold it up a minute," Sanchez said.

"I just want to jump off this rock," Joey said.

"Well, can't you see Collins is going to dive?"

"Aw, he's just going to stand there. He's not going to make a dive. He's putting you on."

I swung my arms, bent my legs, and leaped straight out with all my might. I seemed to pause in the air for an instant. Then I ducked my head and felt a tremendous splash. I scooped with my hands and popped to the surface. I heard Sanchez laugh. Dunnigan cheered and clapped his hands. I climbed out of the water.

"Well, how did that look?"

"I thought you'd konk your head for sure," Dunnigan said.

"Your legs got all bent at the knees," Sanchez said.

"Yeah, but I didn't even hit bottom."

"Far as I'm concerned, Collins, you can have that big old rock all to yourself," Dunnigan said.

"Well, tomorrow I think I'll dive off the Wall."

"Off the Wall? You mean into the deep hole up there?"

"Sure, it can't be too tough," I said.

"Might be a little different diving up there," Sanchez said.

"Well, it's the same kind of water, isn't it? And I won't have to worry about hitting bottom."

"You might be right, but I don't know," Sanchez said.

The next day we practiced our swimming and finally got around to diving off boulders.

"I think I'll dive off the Wall," I said.

"I was wondering when you were going to remember about that," Dunnigan said.

"I was just waiting to feel in shape for it."

"I guess it won't hurt to look it over," Sanchez said.

Dunnigan, Sanchez, and I marched up the road to where the big kids were. We stood at the Wall and looked down. I studied how the river came roaring into the Wall and made an abrupt right turn. The water foamed and splashed and bubbled up in great swirling patterns before it smoothed out and dropped down to the broad pool below. I stepped up to one of the big kids.

"Where do you dive when you dive off the Wall?"

"Well, you see where the water's bubbling there out and down from that big rock? You see how the water seems to rise as it comes up?"

"Yeah, I see it."

"Well, that's a deep hole, and a guy won't hit a rock when he dives in there. But he might not be so lucky if he dove too far on either side of it."

"Are you sure about that?"

"Well, sure I'm sure," the big kid laughed.

I stepped up on the Wall and looked down at the swirling water. It was enough to make me dizzy. I half imagined that the Wall was moving like a giant ship through the water. I flexed my knees to be sure of my footing.

"You mean to tell me he's really going to dive off the Wall?" the big kid asked.

"Well, can't you see he's fixing to?" Sanchez said.

I waited for a few seconds, but nobody said anything. Then I tilted myself off balance, circled my arms, and dove out and down. I hung in the air and saw I was going to hit the spot I was aiming for. I ducked my head and reached with my arms.

The next thing I knew I was tumbling head over heels deep in the turbulent water. I struggled to get upright and started a furious dog paddle for the surface. The water was roaring in my ears.

I broke the surface and water splashed in my face. I sputtered and got a breath. Then I ducked my head and battled the swirling water with my overhand crawl stroke. The swift current swept me into a calm spot behind a big rock at the base of the Wall. I managed to get on the rock and climb back up the Wall.

"What'd you think about that dive?" I asked.

"Holy mackerel, I thought you'd never come up," Dunnigan said.

"I guess my legs flopped some . . . right, Pancho?"

Sanchez looked down at the roaring torrent below us.

"I'd say that was a pretty good dive."

When I told Mother I knew how to swim, she was very pleased. I told her I could swim across the river any time I felt like it and I could do some pretty good dives. She said she was glad she didn't have to worry anymore about me being down at the river.

14

I walked by McGlauflin's Market and looked at my reflection in the first front window. I saw how tall I was and noticed my muscles where my wet T-shirt clung to my chest and arms. I was carrying a rolled up towel.

As I passed the second front window, I glanced at my reflection again, but it was different this time. I was much smaller and bent over a little as I plodded along. I was wearing jeans and a green shirt with long sleeves. I was carrying a metal telescope pole. Four years ago, when I was first trying to be a fisherman, I saw that same reflection many times. I carried that telescope pole a hundred miles or more and only caught four or five trout with it. I was lucky I didn't have to keep on using that old pole, and I thanked Old Mr. Pennyworth for that.

I met Old Mr. Pennyworth as my first summer in Dunsmuir came to an end. All that summer Mother and Father had been trying to find us a better place to live. Finally we moved into a duplex at the north end of town. We rented from Old Mr. Pennyworth and his wife, and they lived comfortably in the other half of the big house which stood next to the highway just below the entrance to Shasta Retreat.

I walked to the edge of the embankment behind our new home and looked down. Through the trees I could see the roof tops of the cabins and vacation homes, and I could see the river. I thought I would go fishing, for there was still time for fishing. I got my telescope pole, my gear, and Mother's permission before I headed down to the river.

In the days that followed I got used to my new home by fishing the river. One day I got lucky again. I had gone down to the Bend and was working my way upstream when I hooked a big trout. It came splashing right up at my feet. I grabbed the trout and held it for a moment. I had forgotten that such a thing could happen.

I took the big trout home and proudly put it in the sink. Mother told Mrs. Pennyworth and Mrs. Pennyworth told Old Mr. Pennyworth. He came over to take a look.

"That's a trout, all right. If you had a dozen more like it, you would have something."

"But it's nine inches long. I measured it."

"I know. Maybe someday you'll catch a big trout, and then you'll know what a big trout is."

That was all Old Mr. Pennyworth had to say.

I went fishing a few more times, but nothing happened. Mostly I was content to do a little exploring and look around for some trees to climb. A grove of cedar and oak trees stood just beyond the large rectangle of lawn that spread out from the Pennyworths' side of the house. The trees weren't too big, but they were close together and right for climbing in.

I played a game to see how many trees I could get into without touching the ground. I usually started by climbing halfway up the biggest cedar tree. From there I jumped across to another cedar. After I got my footing, I leaped straight out and grabbed the big limb of an oak tree. I swung a leg up over the branch and climbed a little higher. Finally I dove straight into the top of a small cedar which bent over as I swung down and dropped to the ground.

I spent many long afternoons playing climbing

games, but the day came I had to go to school and start the sixth grade, and I forgot about the trees.

15

The mornings grew frosty. Sometimes when I went out to catch the school bus, I noticed that the ridges were lined with white. Then one night the snow started to fall. In the morning all of Dunsmuir awoke under a blanket of snow a foot and a half deep.

When I got home from school, Mother told me that the Pennyworths would certainly appreciate me shoveling off their front walk. I got the shovel and went to work. I spent a long time attacking the big pile of snow that the snowplow had pushed up along the side of the highway.

I was cold and wet up to my pockets when Old Mr. Pennyworth opened his door and told me to come in. I propped up the shovel and walked in.

"Stand over there by the fire and dry off," Old Mr. Pennyworth said.

The Pennyworths had a large stone fireplace and several big slabs were roaring away. I backed up to the fireplace and felt a welcome blast of heat.

"You just dry off now and finish shoveling that walk tomorrow," Old Mr. Pennyworth said.

"I can finish it now."

"You just do as I tell you. If you're going to be shoveling off my walk all winter, I want to be sure you don't catch cold and get sick."

"Oh."

Old Mr. Pennyworth was sitting at a table and working with stacks of papers. He seemed to be adding up columns of figures, but I couldn't really tell what he was doing. He finally looked up.

"So you want to be a trout fisherman."

"I think I will be a great trout fisherman."

"Good," Old Mr. Pennyworth said, "but to be great at anything requires dedication and honest hard work, and to be a great trout fisherman requires a pure heart."

"Oh."

I really didn't know what else to say. The back of my Levis were steaming hot. I turned around to face the fire and had to be careful that the back of my legs didn't touch the hot denim.

"Of course you can't be a great trout fisherman with that old telescope pole. You'll have to get a bamboo fly rod."

"How am I going to do that?"

"I don't know, but that's what you've got to have to start."

"Can you teach me to be a great trout fisherman?"

"I can try, but whether or not you're a great trout fisherman is up to you. We can talk about it if you want to."

"Were you a great trout fisherman?"

"I grew up in these mountains. Back when I was a young man, the limit was fifty trout. I could catch fifty trout any day I went fishing. Around that time I was a lumberjack."

"You were a lumberjack?" I backed away from the fire and turned around again.

"I was a tree topper . . . one of the best. I had a world of nerve, and my body was as strong as new wire, but I had to be right. I always felt the moment of truth when that tree top cut loose. Then I would be swaying back and forth at the top of that pole maybe a hundred feet in the air. I can't describe the feeling, but I would just hang there for a long time and look out at the mountains all around me. Sometimes the crew boss would get mad and yell at me to come down, but it was worth it. A man never forgets something like that."

Old Mr. Pennyworth paused for a long moment. He didn't say anything. A strange light shone in his eyes, and he seemed to gaze off into space. I could tell by his look that in his mind the years had fallen away, and he was back swaying in the wind and looking out at the beautiful mountains.

"That sounds like a great thing to do," I said.

"I thought you would understand." Old Mr. Pennyworth smiled slightly as he looked at me. "When I watched you playing in our trees, I could see you were a born climber."

"I didn't know you were watching me."

Mrs. Pennyworth came out of the kitchen. She stood beside Old Mr. Pennyworth and put a hand on his shoulder.

"Pennyworth, maybe this would be a good time to advise Leif not to climb trees," she said.

"I suppose . . . but you know how hard it is to keep a boy out of trees."

"I know how hard it was to keep you out of trees."

"Well, now." Old Mr. Pennyworth laughed and reached up to hold Mrs. Pennyworth's hand which was still on his shoulder. "I don't remember it being all that hard for you."

"Well, I can understand why you like to watch Leif climb trees, but I do worry."

"I know."

"What would I tell Mrs. Collins if her boy hurt himself climbing our trees and we could have prevented it?"

"You're right of course. I think Leif will understand," Old Mr. Pennyworth said.

Mrs. Pennyworth gave him one more pat on the shoulder before she went back to her cooking. Old Mr. Pennyworth looked at me for a moment.

"Actually I'm rather partial to those trees," he said. "I don't want the branches getting broken, and that small cedar never will grow straight if it gets bent over too much."

"I understand."

"Besides, if you're going to do crazy things, don't do them around where people will get worried."

"Did you do crazy things when you were a kid?"

"I'd rather not say." Old Mr. Pennyworth smiled slightly. "You've already got enough ideas."

"Well, what else did you do besides be a lumberjack?"

"Oh, a lot of things. Sometimes I was gone away, but I was always mighty thankful to see these mountains again."

"I expect so."

"I remember once I was gone quite a spell. When I got back, the first thing I did was grab my fishing pole. I went down to Soda Springs and caught fifty trout as slick as ever just to make sure I hadn't lost my touch. As I was coming out the road, the game warden stopped me. He seemed to think I had a lot of trout. I told him I had a limit and he was welcomed to count them, because there wasn't but fifty.

He just laughed and said he was sure I was right. Then he told me the limit on trout had been cut down to twenty-five. Holy smoke, was I embarrassed. He thought that was pretty funny. I sure was lucky he knew who I was. He said he didn't have the heart to do anything but warn me, because he knew I'd been away. And I mean to tell you I never caught more than twenty-five trout after that, and let that be a lesson to you. If you're going to be a great trout fisherman, you'll have to fish by the rules. You had better know the rules before you go fishing."

"You think I'll be able to catch twenty-five trout?"

"I expect you will," Old Mr. Pennyworth said. "I can tell you enough so when everybody is catching trout, you'll get a limit."

"No kidding?"

"No trick to that, but in the middle of the summer when nobody is catching anything, a great trout fisherman can go down to that river and get a limit. That's what's hard to learn, and I can't help you there. You have to learn for yourself, and that might take years."

"That would be worth it."

"Good," Old Mr. Pennyworth said. "Now I'd best get back to these figures. You get home to supper. Tomorrow after you finish shoveling the walk, we can talk some more."

"Thank you," I said. "I'll see you tomorrow."

As I went out the front door, I couldn't help taking a look at the trees across the yard. I knew I wouldn't be climbing any more trees there.

At supper I told Mother that Old Mr. Pennyworth said I would need a bamboo fly rod if I was going to be a great trout fisherman. Mother considered that fishing season was a long time away, but I said a bamboo fly rod was an important thing to have. Finally she said that we would see.

After school the next day I finished shoveling the Pennyworths' walk and knocked at the door.

"Come in, come in!" Old Mr. Pennyworth shouted. I entered and Old Mr. Pennyworth waved me over to the fireplace. He was holding some sheets of paper. I watched as he worked with the papers for a while. Then he looked up. "Well, I suppose you want to talk about trout fishing?"

"Yes," I said.

That afternoon Old Mr. Pennyworth told me some fine stories. He loved to talk about trout fishing, and he loved to talk about people. After that I got into the habit of visiting Old Mr. Pennyworth. He was always doing something with books or papers, but he was never too busy to tell me about things while I dried out in front of the fireplace.

16

A few weeks before Christmas we got our tree. Father got it to stand up straight, and I helped him hook up the lights. Mother let me put the star on the top. Then Mother and I decorated it with ornaments and streamers. I spent a long time putting the shiny icicles on all the branches.

I told Mother again that I would need a split bamboo fly rod if I was going to be a great trout fisherman, but Mother said it was much too soon to think about fishing season.

A week before Christmas Mother spread white tissue paper under the tree and brought all the brightly wrapped presents out of her closet and placed them around under the tree. They looked nice, but I didn't see a package the size I was looking for. Mother was watching me.

"Is something wrong? Don't the presents look nice?" She looked at me and smiled.

"Well, yes." I started to peek into her closet, but she quickly closed the door.

"Oh, no," she said. "That's all the presents now, and I don't want you digging around in my closet."

Naturally I thought there was still hope that I might get the present I was hoping for, but I would have to wait until Christmas Eve to find out. I knew Mother would enjoy keeping me in suspense until the last minute.

Finally Christmas Eve came, but Father had been called out early. He was working the extra board and getting a lot of work. Mother held off dinner and we waited to see if Father would get in late that evening. Sure enough he came in the kitchen door just about the time we were about to give up.

"We doubled right back from Ashland," he said. "I knew I'd make it."

Mother got dinner set while Father went to clean up. After dinner we went into the living room to open presents. Then I saw a package about three feet long propped against the wall behind the Christmas tree. The slender package was wrapped in green tissue paper and had a red ribbon tied around it. Mother smiled when she saw me catch sight of it, but she had Father hand out the presents, and he hardly seemed to notice the one behind the tree.

"What about the present behind the tree?" I couldn't keep quiet about it any longer.

"I guess we better let him open it," Mother laughed.

Father handed me the package. I could feel what it was. I unwrapped it quickly and from the long cloth container withdrew the sections of a bamboo fly rod.

It had a beautiful cork handle with a metal part on the bottom end for the reel. There was a screw adjustment to hold the reel tight. The shafts were shiny with varnish and the eyes were tied with brightly colored thread. The metal sockets and ferrules at the ends of the sections were shiny new.

"Look, it even has an extra tip section!" I said. Mother laughed.

"We were planning to get you a pole before fishing season opened, but I didn't think Christmas would be such a good time."

"Oh, no, this is perfect. Thank you."

"I mean it will be over four months before you'll be able to use it."

"But this is just what I needed. Now I know I'll be a great trout fisherman."

Mother just laughed and shook her head. She couldn't understand me not taking any interest in any of my other presents. I just kept looking at my bamboo fly rod. Then I thought to fit the sections together.

"Don't try to put it together now," Father said.

"Old Mr. Pennyworth said for you to bring it over to him tomorrow, and he will show you how to put it together and take it down the right way."

The next morning as soon as Mother would let me I went to show my bamboo fly rod to Old Mr. Pennyworth.

"It's a beauty . . . take a look." I handed the pole to him.

"Uh huh." He carefully untied the cloth carrying case and withdrew the sections of split bamboo. He looked at the brand name on the bottom section. "Uh huh, they make a good sturdy pole."

"Is it hard to put together?" I watched as Old Mr. Pennyworth started to assemble the pole.

"You have to twist the sections as you put them together . . . and make an allowance so the eyes will be lined up. Don't put a lot of pressure bending the sections, and don't grab onto the eyes either. These sockets will be tight at first, so you'll have to be careful."

"I'll be careful."

Old Mr. Pennyworth got the pole together and stood up to test it. He held it out halfway down the length of the living room and flicked his wrist. The pole whipped back and forth. Mrs. Pennyworth stepped out from the kitchen.

"Pennyworth, what in the world are you doing?"

"Leif got a bamboo fly rod for Christmas." Old Mr.

Pennyworth snapped the rod up and down for emphasis.

"I already know about that," Mrs. Pennyworth said, "but be careful, or you will knock something over."

"Don't worry. We're just testing out the feel of it."

"Well, I hope you boys will remember there's no open season on lamps around here," Mrs. Pennyworth said, and she went back into the kitchen.

Then Old Mr. Pennyworth took the pole apart. He undid the sections with a twisting motion.

"These sockets let loose with a jerk. Be sure you don't jam the tip into a tree or a rock when you're taking it apart."

"I'll watch out."

"Okay, let me see you put it together." He handed me the sections.

With much effort and under Old Mr. Pennyworth's watchful eye I managed to assemble the pole. I stood up and tested it as I had seen Old Mr. Pennyworth do.

"Watch out for that lamp," he said.

"Don't worry. This pole sure is light, and it has a lot of spring to it."

"Actually it's a little bit stiff, but that's just right for you to start with. It'll make a nice bait pole."

I carefully took the pole apart, and Old Mr. Pennyworth put the sections back in the cloth case.

71

"You really think it's a good pole, huh?" I asked.

"Yes sir, you've got just the right pole. You'll catch trout for a lot of years with this pole."

"You really think so?"

"I'm sure of it."

"What else will I need?"

"Well, the pole's the main thing. The rest doesn't amount to much. You sure don't need any fancy reel. Just get yourself a two-dollar reel, but see it has a button on it, so it will click."

"Uh huh."

"Then you'll need some line and a couple of small spools of leader material. I'd say to get around six pound test."

"Okay."

"Get some gold hooks with the short shank. Size ten is about right, and you'll need a couple of packages of split BB shot for sinkers."

"Is that all?"

"That and a jar of pale salmon eggs will do it. Be sure to get the palest salmon eggs you can find, because that's important. But you've got plenty of time for all that, and we can talk about it later."

That afternoon I took my bamboo fly rod and carefully put it up high where little Thor, who was just learning to walk at that time, wouldn't be getting into it.

Then I was back going to school, and the months

rolled by, but every now and then I would get down the fly rod, look at it, and practice putting it together and taking it apart.

17

I skipped across the next intersection. A big cherry tree stood in the front yard on the corner. Several limbs stretched out above the sidewalk. Early that summer I had jumped up and picked off a lot of ripe cherries. Cherry season was always the first great thing to happen after school let out.

As I walked under the overhanging cherry branches, I remembered the time I helped Mrs. Pennyworth pick cherries from the Pennyworths' tree, but that happened after I experienced some of the ups and downs of learning to fish for trout.

18

        In late April I went down to the Big Liquor and Sporting Goods store and got the rest of the fishing equipment that Old Mr. Pennyworth told me about. Then I went straight to his front door and knocked. Old Mr. Pennyworth yelled for me to come in. As I entered, he pointed for me to sit on the couch. He was studying a sheet of paper, and Mrs. Pennyworth was looking over his shoulder.

        "Well, that's the list," Old Mr. Pennyworth said. "Wait a minute, I can't call her. She was involved with the man. Everybody knows that."

        "Well, her name is on the list, and she would want to serve," Mrs. Pennyworth said.

        "Of course, but she'd just be disqualified, and I know Jenkins. He would just embarrass her as much as he could. I'll juggle her name down the list."

"You shouldn't do that. You know that's not right. She should be called and disqualified."

"Hang it all, I'm not going to cause anybody needless embarrassment when I know better. And that's my final word on it."

"Well, it is up to you," Mrs. Pennyworth said, and she went into the kitchen.

"Let that be a lesson to you," Old Mr. Pennyworth said, and he pointed a finger at me. "Sometimes it's wrong to do the right thing, especially when doing the right thing is the easy way out. That's usually when people are involved. Believe me, it's hard to be right when people are involved. That's the hardest thing of all to learn. You'll be lucky to learn that in a whole lifetime. Well, what do you have in the bag?"

I showed the things that I had bought to Old Mr. Pennyworth, and he was pleased to see that I hadn't forgotten anything. He looked the reel over and said it would do just fine. He showed me where to tie the line onto the reel. Then he carefully unrolled the line, so it wouldn't get twisted, as I cranked it onto the reel. Finally he showed me how to make the loop in the end of the line.

"Now I'll make a leader for you," he said, "and you watch closely, because this is important."

Old Mr. Pennyworth took a spool of leader material and strung out as much as he could reach with his arms outstretched. He cut off the piece and showed me how to make a loop again in one end. Then he tied a hook to the other end.

"You see how the hook's tied?"

"Uh huh," I nodded.

"You see how the shank is a continuation of the leader and straight to it?"

"Yes."

"That keeps the barb pointing straight up, so with the least little snap of the pole you can set the hook straight into the trout's mouth."

"I see."

"Now get me the pliers from the kitchen."

I went into the kitchen, and Mrs. Pennyworth found the pliers for me. I thanked her and took them to Old Mr. Pennyworth.

"You'll need at least two split shot sinkers to take the line down, especially since the river is high. I'll just estimate the right spacing here." He squeezed the first split shot onto the leader several inches up from the hook. "That's about right. You don't want to squeeze too hard, or you'll weaken the leader." He squeezed the second split shot a few inches above the first one.

"Is that it?"

"Yes, that looks about right to me. There has to be enough space between the hook and the first sinker so that when you get the line down to where the trout are, the egg has plenty of slack to move naturally in the current."

"That'll fool them."

"Those trout aren't so easy to fool."

"I know that already."

"Of course you're going to fool a lot of them when the season opens."

"You really think so?"

"Sure . . . but it'll get tougher later on."

"I guess so."

"Well, that's enough for now. You take your things home and study that leader. Measure it and measure exactly where the sinkers go. That's important. Bring everything over the night before opening day, and we'll get you all set to go."

"I sure will."

The last day of April was a day of great anticipation for me. After supper I took my pole and all my equipment and went over to see Old Mr. Pennyworth. We sat on the couch and made leaders. He checked my work and showed me how to coil a leader so it wouldn't get tangled. We made half a dozen and put them in a pocket of my fishing bag.

Then he had me put my pole together, attach the reel, and rig the line. I took out a leader and looped it to the line. Old Mr. Pennyworth opened my jar of salmon eggs and showed me how to put an egg on the hook. Finally he made me stand in the middle of the room and show him how I would cast, how I would hold the line away from the pole as I moved the pole to follow the drifting line, and how I would flick up the end of the pole to set the hook.

"Good," he said. "Now do it again."

Mrs. Pennyworth, who was doing some sewing at the other side of the living room, looked up.

"Pennyworth, are you sure all this is necessary? He's going to hook something here."

"Hang it all, of course this is necessary. He's got to know the fundamentals."

"He has all day tomorrow to practice trout fishing."

"This part has to be automatic. He's got a whole lot more than this to learn. This is just a start."

"Pennyworth, I can't tell which one of you is more excited about learning to fish." She laughed and looked back to her sewing.

"Now do it again, Leif," Old Mr. Pennyworth said.

I carefully pretended to cast. Old Mr. Pennyworth told me I would have to learn to watch and feel the movement of the line. Sometimes a smart old trout would just mouth the egg for an instant. If I wasn't ready to flick the end of the pole to set the hook, that old trout would just spit it out. Old Mr. Pennyworth made me stand there for a long time and move my pole slowly across the living room while he explained the art of hooking a trout.

Finally he said I had done enough. He said I had better get to bed early if I was going to get up at first light. I asked when that would be, and he reckoned about five in the morning. Under his watchful eye I dismantled my pole and stowed my gear.

"Now don't be afraid to get your feet wet. Just wear your gym shoes, and wear some dark clothing so you'll blend in with the background. Everything like that helps."

"I hope so."

"Whatever you do, don't make a lot of noise or turn over any rocks on your way down to the water, or you'll just spook those trout."

"Uh huh." I nodded my head.

"Try to cover a long stretch of river and work your way upstream as you fish. Those trout face upstream, and you'll have a better chance if you sneak up behind them."

"I'll stalk those trout."

"Well, do your best, and I'll see you tomorrow," Old Mr. Pennyworth said as I got ready to leave.

"Thank you. I'll see you tomorrow." I closed the door behind me.

The night was pitch black and starry. I hurried into our side of the house and told Mother I would have to use the alarm clock. I got out an old green wool shirt to wear. I put everything on the floor right by my bed. I left my Levis all scrunched up so that I would be able to step right into them. Then I set the alarm for four in the morning and got into bed. I spent a long time thinking about all the things Old Mr. Pennyworth had told me.

I must have fallen asleep, because the next thing I knew the old alarm clock started to ding, and I grabbed it. I strained my eyes to see the hands. It was four o'clock all right. In a rush I remembered all I had to do and jumped out of bed.

The room was dark and cold. I shivered as I struggled into my wool shirt. I stepped into my Levis, zipped them up, and put on a clean pair of wool socks. I was starting to wake up and took my time lacing up my gym shoes. I methodically gathered all my gear together and slung my fishing bag over my shoulder. I made sure I had everything before I slipped out the front door.

19

The night was still pitch black, and I blinked my eyes trying to see better. No cars were on the highway and all was quietness. I could hear the soft rushing sound of the river flowing somewhere below. I walked alongside the highway and then angled down the road into Shasta Retreat.

Big oak trees arched over the road, and I felt as if I were walking into a black hole. I had to be careful to stay on the road and not bump into anything. I strained my eyes and almost felt my way down to the river.

All was blackness and the sound of the river roaring past me. I stopped to think about where I should be to start fishing at first light. I decided to cross the Shasta Retreat bridge to the other side of the river where I could walk downstream along the railroad tracks until it was light enough to fish. Then I could fish my way back upstream as Old Mr. Pennyworth had told me to do.

I thought the plan a good one, but I shivered and the hair on the back of my neck stood up as I inched my way across the bridge in the cold blackness with the river roaring under me.

I felt more at ease walking along the railroad tracks. The shiny steel rails glistened dully in the darkness. I walked as fast as I could without stumbling over the ties and started to warm up a little. A thin line of light began to show at the eastern rim of the canyon, but the canyon was still dark, and below me the river roared out of a pit of blackness.

I marched along, and slowly the grayness of dawn seeped down. First light was almost on me, and I started thinking again about all Old Mr. Pennyworth had told me. I went around a big bend in the railroad tracks and saw the cement highway bridge far ahead. It was etched in the morning sky. I stopped.

If I started fishing just here and on up to the Shasta Retreat bridge, I would probably be the first person to fish this stretch of river. The very thought excited me. I looked down at the river and could just barely make out the rushing waters and the tangle of brush below me. I started down very carefully. I didn't want any rocks breaking loose and upsetting the trout.

I finally found a spot near the water where I could set up my pole. I could just see what I was doing, and the coldness swirled over me again. I shivered. I spent a long time threading the line and making sure everything was right. I opened the jar of salmon eggs and put an egg on the hook.

The river was high and swirling rapidly. The sound of it rushed into my ears. There were some rocks upstream, but the water was splashing over them. Branches of brush were dipping into the high current. The water looked deep. I studied how it eddied and smoothed out slowly just before it dropped down into the rapids below. I inched closer, let out some extra line, and planned my first cast.

I swung the salmon egg far out and up where the water came splashing over the rocks. The line moved swiftly, and I was quick to take up slack and raise the pole as I followed the movement. Nearly all the leader was underwater and moving smoothly with the current. Then the line slowed and seemed to swirl into an undercurrent. My arms were tense, and I strained my eyes to keep track of the line.

I felt a slight tug, and my whole body reacted to jerk the pole straight up. The line zigzagged for an instant, and the pole bounced in my hand. Almost before I realized I had hooked a trout, the fish broke the surface. I kept the pole high as the trout splashed across the water and landed on the rocks at my feet. I grabbed the trout quickly. It was a good eight to nine inches long. I was amazed. My hands shook slightly as I unhooked the trout and dropped it into my fishing bag.

I had to get down to business and compose myself for another cast. This time I cast farther out and closely followed the movement of the line into the deep swirling water. Again I felt a bite and snapped up the end of the pole to hook another trout. This one I played more smoothly in against the shallow rocks where I could reach down and hook a finger through its gills. It was just as big as the first one, and I quickly had it in my bag.

I was feeling very good, but I concentrated on being methodical. After all, I had a long way to go to catch a limit. I made a few more casts and caught another trout almost as big as the first two. Then after I made several casts without getting a bite, I remembered Old Mr. Pennyworth saying I must keep moving and cover a lot of river if I wanted to catch trout.

I was eager to get to another spot, but it was tough going through the brush, and I had to get into the water to get around a bad spot. The water was ice cold and my feet were freezing, but I wasn't going to waste time climbing up and down the embankment to get to another place where there was room to cast.

I caught two more trout behind a big rock and moved upstream again through the brush and in the water. I found a spot where I could wade out just far enough to cast into deep water, and I had more good luck. Then I just kept heading upstream and trying wherever I could even though my feet were getting numb. I was catching a lot of trout, and they were all good-sized. My fishing bag was getting heavy. When I stopped to fish, I would unsling the bag and set it in shallow water to keep the trout fresh.

I lost track of how many trout I caught and thought I should stop to count them. I found a nice spot where there was some grass and room to spread out the trout. I figured on at least twelve or thirteen; but when I had them spread out, I counted seventeen trout. I could only catch eight more. I cut some grass, put it in the bottom of my fishing bag, and carefully laid the trout back in. I took a moment to soak the bag. Then I slung it over my shoulder and started upstream again.

The sun had come up, but it wasn't onto the river yet. I could see the day was going to be bright and warm, but my feet were still numb from the cold. I didn't care. I still kept along the river and waded when I had to. In about an hour I caught eight more trout and stopped to make a final count. Sure enough, there were twenty-five trout. I just sat on a rock and looked at them for a long time.

I could hardly believe I had caught all those trout. The late morning sun was just beginning to angle down to the river, and I already had my limit. I just had to laugh to myself about it. I undid my leader, coiled it, and stowed it in my bag. Then I reeled in my line and carefully took down my pole. I packed the trout back in the bag and soaked it once more before I slung it over my shoulder and started up the embankment.

My legs quivered slightly as I climbed up to the railroad tracks, and I could hardly feel the rocks under my feet. The sun had been beating down on the roadbed and it was warm. As I trudged along, my feet started to tingle as they began to warm up. My fishing bag was heavy on my shoulder, but I felt good. I had to laugh to myself again. I just knew I had to be a great trout fisherman.

20

I still had quite a ways to go to get to the Shasta Retreat bridge. As I walked along, I studied the river below me. I saw a lot of great spots to fish, and I studied how I would fish them. I knew there were a lot of trout down there, but they would just have to wait for another day.

As I crossed the bridge, I spotted a couple of classmates fishing the big hole just above the bridge.

"Hey, Joey!" I yelled. Joey looked up.

"Hey, Collins, where you going?"

"Home to eat."

"You do any good?"

"Oh, I already got a limit."

"No kidding?" Joey put down his pole and came running up the embankment. "Can I see?"

"Sure." I opened the flap of my fishing bag.

"Say, you sure got some beauties."

"Just fair eating size."

"Gee, you got a limit, and it isn't even noon yet."

"Well, I got an early start."

"So did I . . . but I only got five."

"Oh."

"Hey, Billy! Take a look at all the big trout Collins got." Billy came scrambling up to us.

"Hey," he said after he looked in my bag. "Where did you catch all those?"

"I just walked down the tracks and fished part way up the river."

"Hey, Billy, let's go down that way and try," Joey said.

"Aw, Collins must've caught 'em all."

"No, I saw a lot of great spots I didn't even get a chance to try yet."

"No kidding?" Billy asked.

"Sure—but you got to keep moving upstream and fish all the river you can."

"Hey, Joey, let's get going." Billy started back down the embankment.

"Thanks, Collins," Joey said. "See you later."

"Good luck!" I yelled.

As I started up the road out of Shasta Retreat, I started feeling great. I was finally warmed up, and my legs were getting their strength back. I was starting to get hungry. When I got home, I went straight to the Pennyworths' side of the house and knocked on the front door. Old Mr. Pennyworth opened it.

"Well, Leif, how did it go?"

"I got the limit, and it isn't even noon yet."

"Well, let's have a look." Old Mr. Pennyworth managed to step out onto the porch. I opened up my fishing bag as wide as I could while he poked around in it for a minute or two. "Uh huh," he said. "I knew you wouldn't have any trouble opening day."

"Yeah, I caught one on my very first cast."

"I see you caught a lot of hatchery fish."

"Hatchery fish?"

"They stocked the river with a lot of them this year."

"Oh."

"They're kind of soft. You see the ones with the white bellies?"

"Uh huh." I nodded my head.

"Those hatchery fish don't have much of a chance

to get river wise. They'll strike at anything . . . they don't last very long."

"I guess not."

"Did you happen to hook into any big trout?"

"I don't think so."

"Oh, you would have known about it if you had."

"Oh."

"Well, you did catch yourself a mess of trout in short order."

"They're all good eating size, aren't they?"

"They sure are . . . and you better get to cleaning them. That's part of being a fisherman."

"Yeah, I know."

"Good." He started back into the house.

"Would you like to have some trout?"

"No, Leif, I don't eat trout much anymore, but thank you for asking just the same."

"Oh, that's all right," I said. He paused in the doorway and pointed a finger at me.

"You be sure all those trout get used now. That's part of being a fisherman, too."

"Yes, sir."

"We can talk trout fishing later. Right now I've got work to do."

I trudged around back to our side of the house. I felt crushed. I sure didn't feel like any kind of a great trout fisherman. I had only caught a bunch of dumb hatchery fish that would strike at anything. I went in the back door and entered the kitchen where Mother was feeding baby Thor his lunch. He was sitting in his high chair and making his usual mess of it. He waved his arms and babbled when I came in. Mother looked up and seemed surprised.

"You're home early, Leif."

"Yeah."

"Did you catch any trout?"

"Aw, I did all right I guess. Anyway I got a limit."

"You did?"

"Uh huh." I opened my fishing bag and dumped all the trout into the kitchen sink.

"Oh, my goodness," Mother said. "Did you really catch all those trout?"

"Aw, they're mostly just hatchery fish. There's no trick to catching the limit on opening day."

Mother must have noticed that I looked a little depressed. She paused to study me for a moment as I looked down at the sink full of hatchery fish.

"Well, you're the one who caught all those trout, and you're the one who's going to have to clean them."

"Well, I know that. That's part of being a fisherman. Anyway I'll eat some for lunch."

"Fine," Mother said, and she seemed relieved.

21

School didn't let out until a month and a half after the opening of trout season. Most of the time after a school day I would grab my pole and hit the river. I would usually catch five or six trout before it started to get dark. Sometimes on the weekends I would fish all day, and a couple of times I managed to get the limit again.

One Saturday I hiked all the way down to South Dunsmuir and fished all the spots that had been so frustrating for me the year before. I ran into Sanchez and Dunnigan. They were surprised to see I had caught a limit. Sanchez said it was getting tough to catch trout. I had to admit it was getting tougher for me.

By the time school let out, I could go fishing all day and be lucky to catch four or five trout. A lot of kids were saying that the river was all fished out, but I knew better. I just couldn't prove it.

Not long into summer vacation the Pennyworths'

tall cherry tree came ripe with big black clusters of bing cherries. The whole tree was loaded down with them. Early one morning Mother woke me up and told me that Mrs. Pennyworth would appreciate me helping her pick some cherries. I ate a quick breakfast and hurried over to the Pennyworths' side of the house.

"What a beautiful crop of cherries," Mrs. Pennyworth said as we went out to pick them.

"They sure taste sweet," I said, and she handed me a bucket.

"Try to get them in the bucket. Don't let too many of them drop into your mouth."

"Okay."

We had an easy time picking the lower branches, but before long the pickings got slim. Mrs. Pennyworth stood back and looked up at the tree.

"Do you think you could climb up and reach some of the higher branches?"

"You mean it's okay to climb a cherry tree?"

"Only at picking time," she said. "I'll watch you. You will be careful, won't you?"

"Sure."

I climbed up in the tree and reached up and out along the branches to pick as many cherries as I could. The tree was quite tall, and the higher branches hung way out where I couldn't possibly reach them. I finally had to come down.

"I guess that's the best we can do for now," Mrs. Pennyworth said. "I just wish we could get a little higher." We stood there a moment looking up at the tree.

"Those top limbs are really loaded down, but I know they'd break if I tried to crawl out there."

"You did just fine, Leif. Thank you. I'll bring some cherries over to your mother."

"Thanks . . . I've got to go fishing now."

"Okay," she said.

I got a good start and fished all day long, but I didn't catch a single trout. At dusk I trudged up the road out of Shasta Retreat, and I couldn't even remember having any bites. I was discouraged and thinking I was right back where I started from. I was nowhere near being a great trout fisherman.

After supper I sat around feeling depressed. Finally I just felt tired and went to bed. Before I fell asleep, I started thinking about Old Mr. Pennyworth. I knew he wouldn't want me to give up. I decided to see him soon and tell him my tale of woe.

The next morning I remembered I wanted to talk to Old Mr. Pennyworth. I hurried out the front door. As I rounded the side of the house, I saw Mrs. Pennyworth standing on her lawn and looking up at the cherry tree. Then I noticed that a workman had climbed high up into the cherry tree, and he was holding a hand saw up over his head.

"Is this about where you mean?" he asked, and he looked down at Mrs. Pennyworth.

"Yes, I think that'll be just fine."

The workman started sawing, and a minute later the high top of the cherry tree toppled over and tumbled down onto the lawn. Big black cherries bounced around everywhere.

"Beautiful!" I said, and I started picking them up.

"Now, Leif, put them in the bucket." Mrs. Pennyworth went over to pay the workman and thank him for his trouble. He thanked her, got into his truck, and drove off. We were busy gathering the cherries and picking them off the limbs when Old Mr. Pennyworth came out the door and limped slowly down the front walk.

"What in the world have you done to the tree? How could you do such a thing?" he asked. Mrs. Pennyworth and I looked up at the tree and then back at Old Mr. Pennyworth. "Lord Almighty, you had him cut the whole top off the tree. The tree is ruined. It'll never be the same," he said.

"When I asked yesterday, you said—" Mrs. Pennyworth started.

"I thought you would just trim a few branches that might be breaking under the weight, but this is terrible."

"I told you all the cherries were at the top. You said to go ahead and have it done."

"Hang it all, it's not worth spoiling a tree to get a few extra quarts of cherries. We should've let the birds have them. That's what we should've done." Old Mr. Pennyworth started swearing.

"Pennyworth! Control yourself."

"Hang it all, I should've known something like this was going to happen," he said. "I just didn't think. I didn't use my head. How could I have been so stupid?" Old Mr. Pennyworth puffed up his cheeks for a moment and looked all around the yard. "I swear I'll never let anyone cut on another tree around here for as long as I—" He stopped and puffed up his cheeks again. I could tell by the look on his face that a feeling of frustration had come over him. Then he noticed that I was just standing there watching him. He looked at me sharply. "Let that be a lesson to you," he said, and he pointed a finger at me. "You never get too old to make a stupid mistake."

He turned suddenly and made his way back up the walk. He was still muttering to himself as he went in the front door. Then I helped Mrs. Pennyworth pick the rest of the cherries.

I didn't think the time was right to bother Old Mr. Pennyworth with my troubles. I decided to talk to him about my trout fishing when he was in a better mood.

As I said good-bye to Mrs. Pennyworth and started

back home, I glanced up at the cherry tree once more. It looked badly stunted. I had to admit Old Mr. Pennyworth was right.

22

The sound of running water startled me. I turned and saw that I was walking by the Union Oil station. The attendant was starting to hose down the driveway. The cold clear water splashed and sparkled on the concrete. I thought of the river in the sun and of the fact that trout don't have eyelids. Old Mr. Pennyworth told me about it.

"That's why the middle of the day isn't the best time to go fishing," he said. "Trout don't much care for a lot of bright sunlight."

When I complained that I couldn't catch any trout, he looked surprised.

"Hang it all. You must be forgetting everything I told you." He started recounting everything to me all over again, but I kept telling him I remembered everything and I was still doing everything right. I even argued with him about it.

Finally Old Mr. Pennyworth stopped talking. He puffed up his cheeks some, and I could see that he was frustrated. I didn't say anything. I knew what was going through his mind. Old Mr. Pennyworth had been a great trout fisherman, and all that knowledge was right there in his mind, but he was an old man. He could hardly get around anymore. He sure couldn't take me down to the river and show me how to catch those trout.

"Hang it all," he said at last. "I told you I could only give you a start. I told you it might take years to learn to be a great trout fisherman."

"That's true."

"I told you that you would have to learn it on your own. That's the only worthwhile way of learning a thing anyway."

"I guess I was just feeling discouraged."

"Well, that I can understand, but you can't let it get the best of you. You've got to start thinking about all the things you've learned. You already know how to do a lot of things right, but you've got to try new things and see what works. You've got to get into that river and learn to think like a smart trout."

"You must be right. I sure haven't been thinking lately." I had to laugh about it.

"That's the spirit, Leif. One thing's for sure. If a fellow was to plant his feet in that river and fish both sides and the middle all the way up to Box Canyon, he would just have to learn a lot about trout fishing. There's the secret of it, if there is one."

"I'll give it a try."

"You might even hook into a big trout."

"You think so?"

"Sure, there's big trout nobody even knows about." Old Mr. Pennyworth got a faraway look in his eyes. "Those big trout like the deep water . . . where it's dark and cold . . . way down out of sight. You'd never know they were there."

That night I lay in bed thinking about all that Old Mr. Pennyworth had told me. Then I started making plans. I was only an eleven-year-old boy, but a lot of old river-wise trout would have been startled that night if they had known how hard I was thinking about them.

The next day I took some allowance money I had been saving up and went down to the Big Liquor and Sporting Goods store. I bought a jar of their palest salmon eggs and a dozen size twelve, short shank, gold hooks. I had been using the larger size ten. Then after much debate I bought two small spools of thin, three-pound-test, leader material.

I spent that afternoon making extra long leaders. I put the split shot a little farther up from the hook than I usually did. I packed everything into my fishing bag and added a couple bags of salted peanuts.

After supper I went over to talk to Old Mr. Pennyworth, but he was busy working on some books. I just had time enough to say I was going to get up at first light and catch some trout. He said that was a good idea and wished me luck.

I borrowed the alarm clock from Mother and said I would have to get up early if I was going to get in any good fishing. She seemed surprised that I was going to bed so early. I set the alarm for four in the morning. After I said my prayers, I just lay there reviewing everything about trout fishing. I thought I never would fall asleep. Then I imagined myself down in the river. I was wading along and making long casts. I watched the line moving slowly and smoothly in the current. I waited for the trout to strike. Then I fell asleep.

The alarm rang and I stifled it quickly. I sat up to get my bearings. It was still dark. I got dressed quietly, picked up my gear, and went softly out the door. All was quiet.

"The early bird gets the trout," I said to myself as I headed down into the dark shadows. I went straight to the river and stopped to set up my pole and thread the line. First light was just beginning to show. I baited the hook, and I was ready. I yawned and then waded right into the river. The shock of ice cold water on my feet woke me with a shiver. I got down to business and made my first cast. Nothing happened.

"Well, what did you expect?" I asked myself, but I spoke in a whisper and made another cast. Again nothing happened. I made a lot of casts and nothing happened. Then I started upstream. I waded whenever I could and made one cast after another. I kept swinging that egg out and gently dropping it into the water. I wanted to cover the whole river.

"A smart trout might be anywhere," I whispered to myself. "A smart trout is where you find him." Where the river widened I waded out to the middle.

"Both sides and the middle," I whispered and made the casts. Then the unexpected happened. My pole dipped sharply, and the line zigzagged through the water. I gradually realized I had hooked a trout, but I just stood there like an uninterested observer.

"Well, what do you know about that?" I whispered. I had an impulse to jerk my pole straight up and bring the trout out of the water, but I hesitated. I knew the light leader would snap if I wasn't careful. I held the pole steady and the line taut as the trout made a run downstream. I managed to turn him, and he started back upstream.

Suddenly he shot to the surface and thrashed madly for an instant trying to shake the hook loose.

Then he dove and buried himself again. He started downstream, but I turned him more easily this time. Now he was fighting against the current and the steady pull of my line. I gradually edged my way into the shallows and eased the trout closer. I saw that the fight was out of him, and I pulled in line until I could reach down and grab him by the gills. He was mine. The trout wasn't as big as I had thought he would be.

"You're just good eating size," I said to the trout, "but you put up a good fight."

23

I slipped the trout into my bag and rebaited the hook. I carefully waded out to where I could try the same spot again. After several casts I gave up. There were no more takers.

I started upstream and made a long cast up and across to the other side of the river. Almost at once I felt a strike and flicked the tip of my pole. I saw the trout flash as he rolled over and got rid of the hook. My empty line shot out of the water, but I almost had him.

I put on another salmon egg and made several perfect casts to the same spot.

"Well, Collins, now why don't you use your head? A smart trout isn't going to give you two chances. If you don't hook him the first time, you can forget it."

I started upstream and came to a broad deep pool. I got out of the water and quietly stalked up along the bank to where I could make a cast into the riffle at the head of the pool. I dropped the egg gently into the riffle and watched it sink and swirl into the deep current. In an instant the line stopped. I flicked the end of my pole and hooked one.

The trout flashed back and forth and took off downstream. I played him back, and he broke the water with a splash. Then he dug down into the deep current. Up he came again with a spinning leap out of the water, and he popped the surface as he splashed in and started downstream.

"Oh," I whispered. I followed him down to the calmer water where I played him into shore and landed him. His gills were gasping, and he was all played out.

"You're a beauty," I said to the trout. "This is a great spot." I stalked the pool again and dropped another salmon egg into the riffle. I waited with great expectation for the line to stop, but it didn't. I cast again and again with no result. I couldn't believe there were no more trout in this hole.

"You're not using your head again, Collins. The one you caught made such a fuss that he spooked the rest." I resigned myself to that fact and started wading upstream again. I didn't think much of this stretch of river, but I just kept casting everywhere whether I thought there were trout there or not. I got some surprises. I got strikes when I least expected them, and I managed to hook two more trout before I got to Mossbrae Falls.

"Well, are you learning anything, Collins?" I started answering myself as I stalked the deep hole at the far side of the falls.

"Those trout are pretty sharp all right. If they see something they like, they are bang right on it. They don't let anything go by they don't want to go by. Every trout I catch and most every strike is on the very first cast. Maybe something might happen on the second cast, but the third cast you can forget it. If you don't fool a smart trout right off the bat, the chances are you won't fool him all day long. If that smart trout does hit that egg and if you don't hook him right then, you can forget that, too."

I was considering a lot of things as I made a cast into the white water at the head of the pool. The egg sank slowly, and I let out more line as the egg drifted down into the deep current. I waited. Then I let out more line. I was just beginning to reel in when I thought I felt something. I gave the pole a tentative flick upward with my wrist.

Suddenly the pole bent, and I held it steady as I watched the line move downstream. The line lifted slowly up from the water, and I saw a trout flash just below the surface at the far end of the pool. He started back up toward me, and I had to haul in the slack quickly to keep the tension on him. Then he broke the surface in front of me, and I saw how big he was.

"Now don't get excited, Collins. Don't get excited." I had to let out more line as he zigzagged downstream again. I played the trout for several minutes until I worked him into a shallow spot where he stopped struggling just long enough for me to scoop him up onto the beach. I just stood there shaking as I watched the big trout flopping in the sand.

"All right, Collins. Now you can get excited." After I got my line all straightened out, I couldn't resist making another cast in the same spot. I wasn't surprised that I didn't get another bite. I reeled in the line.

I washed off the big trout and slipped him in my bag. He didn't look much like a rainbow, but he was the biggest trout I'd caught so far. I ate a bag of peanuts and started upstream. I didn't make more than a couple of casts in any one spot. I just kept moving. I caught two more trout before the sun was on the river. I was wading upstream when I stopped to eat another bag of peanuts.

"Okay, Collins. It looks like this trout fishing is all walking, wading, and climbing through the brush; and that's what it takes to catch trout."

I started off again, and the sun was hot on me. I knew that the middle of the day wasn't the best time for trout fishing, but I just kept on anyway. I got several more bites and managed to land a couple more trout before I stopped to think about it. I just stood there in the middle of the river with the hot sun beating down on me.

"Say, Collins, have you noticed that you got a couple strikes in shady spots? You hooked that last trout when you let the line drift in under that overhanging branch. Yeah, those trout are pretty smart all right. They don't like the hot sun. They're all laying in the shade."

I started off again and paid special attention to shady spots and the dark sides of boulders. I struggled along up past Shasta Springs and caught three more trout. I lost track of how many trout I had, so I finally stopped to count them. I was pleased to find that I already had twelve. Maybe I could get a limit if I kept at it. The going was rough. I was in the water most of the time, and the bites were few and far between.

The river looped around, and above it the railroad tracks curved to follow. I noticed a sign that read "Small" and could see it was the name of a railroad siding. I caught a fair-sized trout and started to concentrate harder on my fishing again. Then I hooked a big trout just below a spot where a little creek came gurgling into the river. The trout had a lot of fight in him, but I finally landed him. He was almost as big as the one I had caught back at the falls

The afternoon sun was off the river now, and I hurried to get in more good fishing. I came to a place of giant boulders, and someone had a summer home just across the river. I caught two fine trout right out of what was almost someone's front yard.

Next came a long stretch of rapids, but I waded right in and kept casting. I finally caught another trout. I was keeping count and knew I had seventeen. The line of sunlight was climbing up out of the canyon, but I just kept looking upriver for the next spot to cast. I caught number eighteen as dusk was beginning to settle along the river. I kept moving and caught my nineteenth trout.

Darkness was coming on. I knew I would have to quit soon. A little farther upstream the river swirled around a big boulder. The water looked deep and dark. I waded out and made one last cast to the edge of the boulder.

I felt a sudden jolt, and my pole dipped sharply. I started to flick the tip up, but the pole almost jerked out of my hand. I managed to let out some line and hold the pole steady. I strained my eyes in the dimness and the biggest trout I'd ever seen rolled to the surface, whipped his tail over, and made a big splash of water. I was stunned.

The trout headed straight into the rapids, and my pole started to bend. I let out more line and tried to start wading downstream, but my footing wasn't good. My pole bent again, but this time the line suddenly went limp. I caught my balance and reeled in the line. The leader was gone. I was trembling all over, and I just stood there looking downriver. I shook my fist and yelled at the trout.

"You're not so smart either! I'll catch you yet. I'll catch you someday!"

The loud sound of my voice startled me. I looked around. I was standing in the middle of the river, and it was nighttime. There were dark shadows all around me, and the stars were coming out. The hair on the back of my neck started to rise. I was far from home and the night was black.

I would just have to climb up to the tracks and follow them back, but there was a tunnel to go through, and I would have to be careful crossing the railroad bridge that crossed the river just above Mossbrae Falls.

24

I did a lot of talking to myself that night on my way home. I recounted the whole day of fishing and even told myself some stories. Then I did some whistling.

At last I was walking up the road out of Shasta Retreat, and I started to get a warm feeling inside me. I was happy to be coming home. I was like an Indian boy who had spent all day fishing far up the river. I had caught many fish for the people. Through the darkness I could see the campfires. Soon I would be sitting at the fire, eating trout, and listening to stories. Then I would fall asleep on a blanket of soft rabbit fur.

I was feeling very satisfied with myself as I stepped in the back door and entered the kitchen.

I saw that Mother and Mrs. Pennyworth were sitting at the kitchen table.

"Well, here's the boy now," Mrs. Pennyworth said.

"Leif, do you know what time it is?" Mother asked. "Didn't you know I'd be worried?"

"Ah . . . I was just fishing."

"I'll just go tell Pennyworth the boy's back," Mrs. Pennyworth said, and she stepped out the door.

"It's after ten o'clock at night, Leif," Mother said. "What was I to think? I was ready to send people out to look for you. If Mr. Pennyworth hadn't been so reassuring, I would have done it. He was sure you'd be back, but I didn't know."

"I'm sorry. I didn't think it was so late until it got dark, and it was a long walk back."

"Leif, I don't want to be angry with you, and I am relieved to see you, but I just want you to remember that I worry about you."

"Yes, Mother." There was a knock at the door, and Mother opened it. Old Mr. Pennyworth and Mrs. Pennyworth came in.

"Well," Old Mr. Pennyworth said. "We were all a bit concerned about you, young man."

"I'm sorry."

"What were you up to?" he asked.

"I was trying to catch the limit, but it got dark

on me. I only got nineteen." I emptied my fishing bag into the sink. Old Mr. Pennyworth stepped over to take a look.

"Uh huh." He poked around in the sink. "You got a nice mess of wild trout, and that's for sure. I haven't seen the likes of this in quite a spell."

"No kidding?"

"Uh huh. Look at here . . . you caught yourself a couple of German browns. Not many of them in the river anymore."

"I thought they looked different."

"Where all were you fishing anyway?"

"Well, I went straight down to the river and got in just like you said and started fishing upstream."

"Just like I said?"

"I kept trying to fish both sides and the middle."

"Oh, now I remember."

"I went up past Shasta Springs and past a siding called 'Small.' "

"Uh huh."

"Then I saw someone's house on the other side of the river, and I kept going from there. I walked the tracks back and had to come through a tunnel."

"Good Lord, you must've fished five miles of river."

"Just before dark I hooked a big trout."

"You did?"

"Yeah, I saw him roll over. He must have been

21 inches long. He made a big splash and went straight into the rapids and took my leader with him."

"That would be a big trout all right."

"How do you catch a trout that big?"

"It takes patience and luck. You don't get a chance at a big trout every day. Even a great trout fisherman has to be lucky to catch a big trout."

"I guess so."

"Well, you did catch a lot of nice solid trout. I bet they put up a good fight."

"They sure did. Would you like to have some?"

"Well, now . . . a couple of them might be tasty for breakfast."

"I'll bring you over some."

"Uh huh," he said. "Now you better get to cleaning."

"Sure."

"Just you remember for next time that you don't have to do all your fishing in one day."

"Yes, sir."

"Hang it all, Leif, we don't want the womenfolk fretting over you all the time, do we?"

"No, sir."

"Okay, then."

Mother walked the Pennyworths to the door, and they stopped just outside to talk for a minute. I was busy cleaning the trout, but I couldn't help overhearing most of the conversation. Mother thanked the Pennyworths and said she was sorry to have bothered them. Mrs. Pennyworth said it was perfectly all right and understandable.

"Now don't you be too mad at the boy," Old Mr. Pennyworth said. "I'm partly to blame myself. I mean to say he's just a natural-born fisherman. If you knew how hard he worked to catch those trout, you would just have to feel mighty proud."

When I heard what Old Mr. Pennyworth said, I couldn't help feeling that maybe I was a great trout fisherman after all. Mother thanked the Pennyworths again and said good night. She came back into the kitchen.

"I suppose I'll have to forgive you this one time, but I'll still have to tell your father when he gets in tomorrow."

I was feeling just like a trout that had flipped over and gotten rid of the hook until she said the last part. Then I knew I wasn't off yet. Baby Thor started to make a fuss, and Mother went to tend him. I had five more trout to clean and got busy with them. Suddenly I got a funny feeling and looked around.

Father was standing right behind me. His lantern was hooked over his arm, and his cap was pushed up high on his head. He seemed to be amused by the look on my face.

"Ah . . . you're home."

"Doubled back from Ashland. Things are pretty busy. I see you caught some nice trout."

"It took me all day. I'm afraid I got home way after dark." Father began to look not so amused.

"You know I don't want you to get your mother to worrying."

"I'm afraid she got a little worried."

"Oh, oh." He took a deep breath and paused to look at the trout. "If you want to be catching any more trout, you better be getting home before dark."

"Yes, sir."

"I'm not going to be telling you about it again."

"I understand."

"You always say you understand. Maybe you understand things too easily."

"I mean I'll remember."

"That might be a help. Where's your mother?"

"Thor started to fuss."

"Oh." He went to put some coffee on.

The next few times I went fishing, I got home way before dark. I didn't even want to cut it close. It did pain me to think that I could get home before dark five hundred times in a row; and if on the five hundred and first time I got home late, they would make it sound like I never could get home on time. Of course I wasn't that good about it, and they did give me a lot of leeway, so it wasn't that big a

bother. It was just one of those little things I had
to live with.

25

I only had to pass a few
more homes to be downtown. The houses were
down and back from the highway, and the front
yards were on a level several feet lower than the
sidewalk. I looked down and noticed someone mowing a lawn. Then I recognized Billy.

"Hey, Billy!" I waved as he looked up.

"Collins! What's doing?"

"It's time to go swimming."

"I got a job mowing lawns. Maybe I'll see you
later."

"Yeah, I'm going to swim until they close the
pool." I waved once more, and then Billy put his
head down again and started pushing the mower.

Seeing Billy reminded me of the swimming season that happened right after I started to learn to
catch trout. I was concentrating on my fishing then

and was excited by the idea I could go down to the river and catch some trout any time I wanted to.

One morning I got up early, hiked down to the roundhouse, and started to fish upstream. I liked to catch those trout while the dew was still on them. I caught six. Then the sun came up like a rocket, and things started to get mighty hot.

I guess I was feeling a little lazy, because I considered heading for home. I got to thinking about a big bottle of strawberry soda I had in the refrigerator, and that did it. I took down my pole and started up the road.

When I got to the Bend, I saw a lot of kids were coming down to go swimming. Some were already at it. I stopped for a minute to watch. Billy was standing on a rock near the water, and he looked up and spotted me.

"Hey, Collins!" he yelled. "It's swimming season." He turned and did a bellyflop into the river. He came up splashing and waving. "The water's great."

"I'll be right back!" I yelled, and I started off in a hurry. I jogged most of the way home and rushed in through the front door. Mother was folding some clothes.

"What's the matter?"

"Time to go swimming. Where are my swim trunks?"

"Leif, you're all out of breath."

"Well, I've been running. I've got to get back."

"Why are you in such a rush?"

"Well, it's already swimming season, and I'm late."

"Late?" Mother asked, and she gave me a certain look that meant she was trying to figure me out.

"Can I go swimming?"

"May I go swimming, please," Mother said. She always made it a point to correct my English when she was trying to slow me down.

"May I go swimming, please?"

"I still don't understand why you're in such a hurry," she said.

"It's just swimming season, that's all. Everybody's down to the Bend right now."

"Well, I don't know," Mother said.

"Anyway I have to clean these trout first." I hurried into the kitchen, dumped the trout into the sink, and put my fishing gear away on the back porch. I was almost finished cleaning the trout when Mother came in.

"Well, I did find your swim trunks."

"Great."

"You'll have to eat lunch first."

"I don't want nothing to eat."

"I don't want anything to eat."

I repeated the sentence correctly and reminded Mother that I had eaten a big breakfast. Then I finished cleaning the trout, wrapped them in foil, and put them in the refrigerator.

"May I please go swimming now?" I asked. "I'll be home way before dark."

"Oh, I suppose so."

I grabbed my swim trunks and rushed in to change. I picked up a towel and headed for the front door.

"Now just a minute," Mother said. "Don't be in such a hurry."

"But you said I could go."

"I just want you to be careful."

"Well, you know how good . . . I mean you know how well I can swim."

"Yes, but I just want you to take it easy." I could tell by her look that she still couldn't figure me out.

"Okay, I will," I said, and I was out the door and jogging alongside the highway.

I started thinking that I should have tried to explain things a little better to Mother, but I guessed that she wouldn't have understood that the start of swimming season was a kind of revelation.

To my way of thinking, if I didn't know what season it was, I wouldn't know what to do; and not knowing what to do was the worst thing that could happen to anybody in the whole world.

26

Swimming season flowed along and became the whole world and all of time to me as one scorching hot day melted into the next. We were a happy little group of kids at the Bend. Our bodies turned as brown as old leather. We played all day in the water like a bunch of otters and never thought about tomorrow.

Sometimes a car would pull up and park at the edge of the road above the Bend, and someone would get out and start throwing coins into the water. We would all hit the water with a big splash and swim pell-mell down after the pennies, nickels, and dimes. Those were fun times. We would all pick up a little change, but the money didn't mean anything. We all got a chance to show off how well we could dive and swim underwater.

One day a shiny new Cadillac stopped on the shoulder of the road above us. A fat man stepped out. He was dressed in a suit, and he had a cigar in his face. He just stood there and waited until he had everyone's attention. He held out his hand. We got into position on the rocks and were ready to dive.

The fat man swung his arm in a smooth half circle and lofted a handful of coins into the air. They pelted the water in front of us as we were all leaning into our dives. We plunged into the water and struggled down to pick the glistening coins from amongst the rocks. Then we burst to the surface for a quick breath of air and went down again.

Finally most of us started to hang onto the rocks to get a breather. The fat man held out his hand again and waited while we scrambled back up onto the rocks. Another handful of coins splattered into the deep current and we were after them. There were even some quarters to be had this time.

At last the fat man held up a big fifty-cent piece and gave us plenty of time to get set. He spun the big coin into the air, and it plummeted into the white water at the head of the deep pool. The race was on, and it was a long struggle. Suddenly Bernie pushed to the surface and yelled that he had it. He swam to a rock and held up the fifty-cent piece to show it to the fat man. The fat man waved. Then he got into his Cadillac and drove off.

Several times that swimming season the fat man stopped by, and once I got the fifty-cent piece. I pushed to the surface and yelled that I had it. I swam to the bank and climbed onto a rock. I held up the coin and waved my arm. The fat man waved back and got into his car. I just stood there and watched as he drove on up to the highway.

Somehow I didn't feel quite right about it. Maybe I thought fifty cents was too much for him to have thrown, but I didn't know why I hadn't wondered about that before.

That night as I was walking home, I started thinking about the fat man again. I didn't know what it was about him that bothered me. I certainly didn't know anything about him at all. I didn't envy him, even if he did own a shiny new Cadillac. I considered that when I grew up, I probably wouldn't want to throw handfuls of coins into the river for kids to dive after. It wasn't because of the money. The money didn't really mean anything.

I just didn't want to be like the fat man. I sure didn't want to get all fat and be wearing a suit all the time and go around with a cigar in my face. I didn't want to stop and throw coins to the kids and think I was doing something. I didn't want to be like that at all.

I always wanted to be the guy diving off the rock and struggling down in the deep current. I always wanted to be pushing up for another breath of air, so I could plunge down under the water again. I always wanted to feel my arms and legs getting tired, my heart pounding, and my lungs bursting for air. That was doing something, and that was the only worthwhile way to be; and if I couldn't grow up to be the way I wanted to be, I just wasn't going to grow up at all.

Swimming season ended as suddenly as it had begun. A day came when we all felt a change in the air, and no one had to say anything about it. When I went home and put my swim trunks away, I felt a touch of sadness. A great time had come to an end.

27

School started and I was in the seventh grade. Those first few days I felt as if a heavy door had slammed shut behind me. We all made the best of it, and our afternoons were full of playing softball.

Mother and Father had saved up enough money to put down on a place of our own, so we bought a duplex in South Dunsmuir. It was near the house we had lived in when we first came to Dunsmuir. The building was just off the highway and below it. A wooden catwalk led to the front stairs. We lived in the top half of the place and rented out the bottom half.

When winter came, I had a lot of shoveling to do. Then it came on snowball season, and after school we would have great snowball fights all through town and down to South Dunsmuir. Sometimes we would split up into armies, build forts, and stockpile snowballs. We planned out some great battles.

I thought up the strategy of the mortar barrage. I got everyone to throw a lot of snowballs straight up into the air. As they pelted down around the guys behind the fort, we would charge to the attack and get in a few good shots before the counterattack.

School dragged on in an ordinary sort of way until spring rolled over the mountains and melted the snow off the ridges. The river ran high, and the sun started to lean harder into the afternoons. Things started to grow.

We all started playing a lot of basketball after school. Most of us had seen all the games up at the high school, and we were making plans to be great basketball players. Every afternoon we would be out on the playground, and we would be playing for the championship. It was a pleasant way of marking time, for we were all looking ahead to the start of trout season.

I thought the month of April never would end. I was a little worried that I might have forgotten everything I had learned about trout fishing. I didn't have Old Mr. Pennyworth living right next door anymore. I couldn't run over and talk to him all the time, so I just started talking to myself about trout fishing, and before long I was remembering everything.

28

A week before the season opened, I went down to the Big Liquor and Sporting Goods store and got everything I needed. I spent a couple of evenings sitting around listening to records while I made up a batch of new leaders.

On opening day I got up in the dark. The river was cold and gray. I hiked down to the end of the yards and started fishing upstream past the old hobo camp. I took my time and tried to catch some big trout. I caught a lot of fair-sized ones as I worked upstream. Then I hooked and landed three beauties out of the deep pool right behind Dunnigan's house. They were all between eleven and twelve inches long and solid fighters.

I moved up to the next broad pool and waded out to make a cast. As the salmon egg floated into deep water, I saw a big trout rise to take it. I was startled. The trout was so big I froze for an instant before I snapped up the end of my pole. The big trout rolled to the surface and turned over with a splash. My line shot out of the water as the hook came loose.

I felt the bottom drop out of my stomach, and my hands started to shake. I just stood there staring in disbelief and wondering how I could fish so badly, and I remembered what Old Mr. Pennyworth told me.

"You don't get a chance at a big trout every day."

I finally composed myself enough to start fishing again. I continued on up to Blackberry Hole and had a limit before the day even started to warm up. A lot of kids were fishing along Blackberry Hole, and Dunnigan spotted me. He saw I had taken down my pole, and he glanced at my bulging fishing bag.

"Hey, Collins, you got a limit already?" he asked.

"Yeah, but I lost a big trout," I said. "I did catch a couple of beauties right behind your house."

"No kidding?"

"Take a look."

"I thought I caught them all out of there. I got four the first thing this morning, but none of them was that big," he said as he looked into my fishing bag.

"There's all kinds of trout in this river now. They're practically bumping into each other."

"Well, if you say so, Collins."

"Hey!" Sanchez yelled as he came trudging down toward us. "I got snagged on a rock and broke my leader off." He held up the end of his line which had only a couple of inches of leader on it. "Now I got to make another leader."

"I got some leaders made up," I said. I reached in my bag for some leaders and handed them to Sanchez. "Here, Pancho."

"Hey, thanks, Collins. You sure you don't need these?"

"Aw, he already got his limit," Dunnigan said.

"No kidding?"

"Yeah," I said. "They're all good-eating size."

"Well, that figures," Sanchez said. "I'll see you guys later. I've got to do some fishing."

"Hey, me too," Dunnigan said. We all said goodbye and I headed for home.

29

I walked downtown and felt how hot it was. Heat waves rose smoothly in the calm air. The highway was Dunsmuir's main street, but very little traffic was on the road. Hardly any people were shopping. The awnings hung limply above the store fronts.

I stopped for a cold drink of water from the fountain in front of Paddy's Place. As I straightened up, I saw the flickering beer sign in the front window; and I recalled the mess of trout I caught for Miss Dove.

When I caught those trout, I didn't know how important they would be. I figured there was no accounting for the way I learned things. I usually went headlong into everything without thinking, and sometimes I was hit with a lesson. I thought how fortunate I was to have bumped into the truth in front of Paddy's Place.

I was getting pretty nonchalant about fishing. I

still had some studying to do to get through the seventh grade, but I didn't care. Every day after school I would hurry home, grab my pole, and try to be the first one to hit the river. I caught so many trout that we got tired of eating them, so we started giving them all away.

One day in class Miss Dove mentioned that she had been hearing a lot about trout fishing and about how good trout tasted, but she hadn't had a chance to try any yet. She knew there must be some good fishermen in her class, and she wondered if one of them could catch her some trout.

"Collins can catch you a whole mess of trout," Dunnigan said.

"Yeah, Collins knows how to catch them," Sanchez said. Then everyone chimed in and said I was the one to do it. Miss Dove looked at me.

"Sure," I said. "I guess I can catch a mess of trout for you all right."

"That would be nice."

I really wasn't worried about having to catch a mess of trout for Miss Dove, and the idea just sort of slipped from my mind. That was usually what happened when I wasn't worried about doing something I was supposed to do.

After school I wandered home, picked up my pole, and walked down to the river. I had gotten out of the habit of taking along my fishing bag. The thing was a bother to have hanging on my shoulder all the time. I just stuck my knife and a couple of extra leaders in one pocket, a jar of salmon eggs in the other, and I was all set.

I caught a couple of trout and stopped to cut a forked stick to string them on. I took my time working upstream. The river was still quite high and not so good for wading. Besides that, the afternoon had turned cool, and I didn't feel like getting my feet in the icy water. I walked up along the tracks and went down to the river when I saw a good spot that was easy to reach. I caught a few more trout, but they were nothing to get excited about.

By the time I got to the Butterfly Avenue Bridge, I only had seven trout, and none of them were much over eight inches long. I thought about going home, but there was still some daylight left, and I decided instead to wander up to the first broad pool above the roundhouse. As I started down to the river, I saw that a couple of kids were already fishing there. I spotted Sanchez.

"Hey, Pancho, what're you doing?"

"Hey, not too good, Collins."

Joey turned and saw me coming down. He noticed the trout I was carrying on the forked stick.

"Hey, Collins, are you catching that mess of trout for Miss Dove?" he asked.

"Naw, these aren't anything." I wondered why I hadn't remembered about the mess of trout for Miss Dove. Joey looked a little disappointed.

"They look pretty good to me," he said.

"I only got seven, and they're not very big," I said. "Sure isn't a mess of trout."

"Oh," Joey said. "Hey, try here, Collins. This is a good spot. I got some bites." Joey reeled in his line and stepped back from the rock he was standing on.

"Yeah," Sanchez said. "There's got to be some big trout out there, but I can't reach them."

"Well, I'll try." I dropped my trout into a shallow spot and stepped out onto the rock. I carefully baited my hook and studied the river.

The swollen river made the pool seem bigger than ever. A lot of water came roaring down the far side and swirled into deep currents down the middle. The near side wasn't very deep, and the shallow water swung around in a half circle back up toward the top of the pool.

I didn't think I could cast out far enough to do much good. I let out a lot of line and swung the salmon egg up and out as far as I could. It dropped in at the edge of the deep water. I didn't think much of the cast, but I let out more line and tried to get the egg to sink into the deep current.

"That's a good cast," Joey said.

"Naw," I said, but I saw a trout flash. I flicked up the end of my pole and hooked him.

"See," Joey said. "You got a nice one." I played the trout easily into the shallow water and flipped him onto the rocks.

"Not much bigger than the rest." I strung him on the forked stick.

"It's a start," Sanchez said. "Catch a few more."

I made a few more casts and caught another one. Then I managed a decent cast and got a sharp strike. I carefully played the trout in to where I could reach down and grab him.

"Hey," Joey said. "That's a big one."

"Pretty good trout," Sanchez said.

"Yeah, it's good eating size."

Early dusk was beginning to filter down along the river, but I was finally interested in catching some big trout. I baited the hook, took a deep breath, and waded into the freezing water. I was up to my thighs in a few steps.

In early spring the river had swirled high through this spot and had thrown a pile of sand along this side of the river. In a few more steps I was out on the sandbar, and it wasn't quite so deep.

I made easy casts now, and I caught a ten-incher. I got even wetter as I played him back in where I could land him. The cold water made me shiver, but

I waded out again and hooked another one.

"Collins, you sure can catch those trout," Joey said.

"This is starting to look like a mess of trout," I said as I hefted the forked stick.

Billy and a friend of his were walking up along the tracks. Sanchez hailed them down to have a look.

"Collins is catching that mess of trout for Miss Dove."

"Oh, yeah," Billy said. "Hey, those are nice."

I waded in again and inched my way a little farther out on the sandbar. Dusk was coming on cold, and I started to shiver again. I made a long cast high up into the fast water. I let out a lot of line as the salmon egg sank and swirled downriver into the deep water. A trout hit the line hard, and I knew I had hooked a real fighter.

The line zigzagged back and forth in the deep current, and I fought to hold him. At last I worked him into the calmer water below me. I waded back to the rocks and played the trout in gently. I hooked a finger under his gills and held him up.

"Now that's a big one," Joey said.

"Nice twelve-incher," Sanchez said. I strung the trout on the forked stick and held up the mess of trout.

"Well, how's that look?"

"Great!" Billy said. "That's a nice mess of trout all right."

"Uh huh." I felt pretty good about it and was ready to quit.

"Catch one more," Sanchez said.

"Well, I don't know if I can."

"Come on, Collins," Sanchez said. "Catch one more big one. I know you can do it."

"Yeah," Joey said. "It's not hardly dark yet."

Then everyone else chimed in, and they all stood there watching as I waded back out into the river. Catching another big trout seemed like a tall order, but I was going to try my best. I inched out along the sandbar until I was up to my pockets in cold water. I made a long cast up into the riffle at the top of the pool. I let out a lot of line and let it float a long way downriver. I wasn't expecting a strike, but suddenly my pole bent, and I felt the strong pull of the line moving through the deep current.

"Oh, oh." My feet started to sink down into the sand, and I didn't know who was going to win this battle. I had to let out more line as I inched my way back up onto the top of the sandbar. I watched the line as the trout pulled it through the water.

The trout headed down and across the river. Then he started back and suddenly angled into the calm backwater, and I knew I had him. I hauled in line and started to wade to the rocks. In the gathering gloom I couldn't quite see how big the trout was, but I saw the line cut through the water as he headed straight back into the deep fast water. I had to let out the line and start all over again.

"Oh, no," Billy said. "He's going to lose him."

"Collins knows what he's doing," Sanchez said. I finally played the trout around into the backwater again, and this time he was all wore out. I waded over to the shallows, worked the trout in close, and plucked him out of the water.

"Nice trout," Sanchez said. "Easy thirteen or fourteen inches I'd say."

"Miss Dove is sure going to be surprised," Joey said.

"Well, that makes it a nice looking mess of trout," I said.

"Sure does," Billy said.

"Well, let's get going, Pancho," I said. "I'm getting cold."

"Okay," Sanchez said.

30

We all walked on up to town, and Sanchez and I said good-bye to the others as we started for South Dunsmuir. The evening was coming on dark and cold. I walked as fast as I could, but my gym shoes were all squishy and full of sand.

As we started to go by Paddy's Place, I noticed the flickering beer sign in the front window. The front door opened, and the fat man stepped out. He was all dressed in a suit, and he had a cigar in his face. He just stood there a moment and looked up and down the street. Sanchez had to cross in front of me to get around him. As I passed by the fat man, I noticed how big his belly was.

"Hey, boy," he said. "You catch that mess of trout?"

"Ah . . . yeah." I stopped and looked up at him. He was eyeing all the big trout dangling from the forked stick.

"Haven't seen a mess of trout like that in a while . . . haven't had any either."

"Hey, Collins, come on," Sanchez said. He had stopped and was waiting for me a few steps farther down the sidewalk.

"How much you want for them?" the fat man asked.

"Ah . . . you mean you want to buy them?" I wasn't thinking he would make an offer, and I was a little surprised.

"Come on, Collins," Sanchez said. "Don't be talking to him."

"I'll give you three bucks for them," the fat man said. He had fished into his pocket, and he was holding up several dollar bills.

"No . . . but how about six dollars?"

"Oh, you want to bargain. I like that." He fished into his pocket again, and this time he held up a five-dollar bill. I didn't say anything, so he started to put the money in my hand. Sanchez marched up to me, and he looked a little bit disgusted.

"You can't sell the trout, Collins. They're for Miss Dove."

"Yeah, I know."

"Mister, these trout aren't for sale," Sanchez said.

"I wasn't talking to you. I was talking to him. He's the one who caught them, isn't he?"

Sanchez marched right up against the fat man. "I said these trout aren't for sale, Mister."

"All right, all right." The fat man backed up a little. "Don't get excited."

"Let's go, Collins." Sanchez hustled me on down the street. "The nerve of that guy," Sanchez said. I suddenly realized how close I came to making a bad mistake.

"Well, I wasn't going to sell them . . . I was just wondering how much he was willing to pay."

"It made no sense you talking to him," Sanchez said.

"Yeah, I know. I guess I was just too curious."

"You shouldn't have thought about it."

"Yeah." Then I said something else to change the subject, but all the time in the back of my mind I was feeling disappointed in myself.

A little farther on I had a vision, and I saw Old Mr. Pennyworth sitting at his table and doing his books while I dried out in front of the fire. Old Mr. Pennyworth paused and glanced up at me. He pointed a finger.

"To be a great trout fisherman you must have a pure heart."

In front of Paddy's Place I was tested and found wanting. I just wasn't thinking. Selling trout was against the rules. Everybody knew that. If it wasn't for Sanchez, I would have let the fat man con me out of the mess of trout for a five-dollar bill.

The trout didn't even belong to me. They belonged to everybody. They belonged to Sanchez and Joey and everybody else who stood by and watched me fishing. They knew I was catching a mess of trout for Miss Dove, and they were pulling for me.

The whole class was counting on me, and I made a promise. I almost gave all that up for a little bit of money. I couldn't believe myself. I couldn't believe how stupid I was. The more I thought about it, the worse it got.

I got home at last and changed into some dry clothes. I took my time cleaning the trout and did a nice job. I left the heads and tails on them, so Miss Dove would be sure to see how big they were. I wrapped the trout neatly in foil and put them in the refrigerator.

That night after I said my prayers, I just lay in bed and wondered if I would ever feel good about myself again. Then I had another vision, and I saw Old Mr. Pennyworth sitting on his couch.

"To err is human," Old Mr. Pennyworth said. "Do you know what that means, Leif?"

"Everybody makes mistakes."

"No, that's not the same thing. When someone says, 'Everybody makes mistakes,' it sounds like an excuse."

"Sure, that's how I've heard it."

"It's not much of an excuse, is it?"

"No, none at all."

"When someone says, 'To err is human,' it sounds different, doesn't it?"

"I see what you mean."

"So what do you make of it?"

"I guess it says something about what's in the human nature."

"Very good," Old Mr. Pennyworth said. "If you keep at it, you might learn to think someday."

"So what does it mean?" I asked.

"What?"

"To err is human."

"Oh, that can mean a lot of things. Of course people don't want to make mistakes. They mostly want to be fair and do the right thing, and they want to be admired for it. That's a part of human nature, too."

"Sure."

"Now a man might do everything right and start thinking he's perfect. He'll start thinking he's better than everybody else. Then he's liable to make a big mistake, and that'll be a shock."

"I guess it would be."

"Such a man would have to accept the fact that he was an ordinary human being, or he would be stuck with a fatal flaw," he said.

"A fatal flaw?" I asked.

"In his character," Old Mr. Pennyworth said. "That's the stuff great tragedies are written about."

"Oh," I said. "So what else does it mean?"

"You've got a whole lifetime to think about such things. Just remember to use your mind, and remember you're human like everybody else."

The vision of Old Mr. Pennyworth gradually faded from my mind. I was alone again under the warm covers and looking out at the darkness of my room.

The next morning when I presented the mess of trout to Miss Dove, she was surprised all right.

"Why, thank you, Leif," she said. "These are such big trout, and so many. I certainly didn't expect you to catch them so quickly. Thank you very much."

"You're welcome." I went to my desk and sat down. Everybody in the class was craning their necks trying to see the trout, so finally Miss Dove let everybody file by her desk and take a look at them.

"Didn't I tell you Collins would catch a nice mess of trout for you?" Dunnigan asked.

"Indeed you did," Miss Dove said.

"I saw him catch that big one," Joey said.

Everybody was feeling happy and proud that Miss Dove was so pleased with her mess of trout, but I just sat there quietly. I guessed that if I were a great trout fisherman, I would be feeling all warm inside now; and I would just say that I had gotten lucky.

Instead, I was thinking that Sanchez was the hero. He was the one who made sure Miss Dove got her mess of trout. I knew I didn't deserve all the credit, but I just had to sit there and take it.

Finally I thought of a couple of things to cheer me up. I was happy that I had met Old Mr. Pennyworth and had spent a lot of time talking to him, and I was happy that Sanchez was a good friend of mine.

Although I had a lot to learn, I had plenty of time to learn it. Of course I would have to do a lot of thinking about things. Maybe someday I would even end up being a great trout fisherman.

31

By the time I got through remembering about the mess of trout for Miss Dove, I was way past the main part of town. My mind had been good company, but now I just felt hot and a little impatient to get to the city pool. I thought I was done with remembering spots, but I walked by a stone post and noticed a stone wall that edged a front yard.

I thought of the time Dunnigan and I were wandering through town. We didn't have much on our minds, but on the spur of the moment we got a great idea of something to do. We made some quick plans and started on our way.

"Oh, no!" Dunnigan said. "I've got to go home first."

"Huh?" I asked.

"I've got a chore to do, and I promised. We just don't have enough time."

"There's always plenty of time for doing something great."

"Are we going to stand here and talk about time?" Dunnigan pointed to his wristwatch. "You know I have to get home."

"Why is it, Dunnigan, that people who are patient and really know how to wait always have plenty of time, and they get everything done?"

"We are going to talk about it." Dunnigan rolled his eyes and looked up at the sky.

"And why is it that people who are impatient and rushing around in a hurry and always looking at their wristwatches never get anything done?" I asked.

"I'm going to get that chore done, and I got to go home to do it."

"Well, can you get out again?"

"Oh, sure. No sweat . . . but it'll take a little while. When I get done, I can come up to your house."

"Wait a minute . . . let me think."

We stopped walking to talk things over. At the edge of the sidewalk was a low stone wall that marked the beginning of someone's front yard. I stepped onto the wall and squatted on my haunches.

"I will wait for you right here."

"You'll what?"

"I will demonstrate for you the art of waiting. The only way to learn about patience is to work at it."

"You mean you're going to sit there all scrunched up like that while I walk all the way home, do my work, and walk all the way back here?"

"What always happens when I tell you I can do something?"

"Well, I'm not going to hurry."

"I don't want you to. I need the practice, and this is a good time for it."

"I just think you're some kind of nut." Dunnigan started off. He looked back just once before he turned the corner and was out of sight.

I had picked a shady spot. I looked out and watched the afternoon sun angling across the trees and houses. I listened for the wind and the sounds of birds. I felt the solidness of the stones under my feet, and my body seemed to melt into a solid motionless form like the stone post next to me.

Then my gaze went out across the canyon, and I studied the far mountainside. Many cars and people passed close by me, but I didn't see them. In my mind I was already on my way down to the river and lost in time.

I climbed quietly down the embankment to the first broad pool above the roundhouse. Everything seemed misty and the air was very still. Then I realized that first light was just beginning to filter into the canyon. I shivered and heard the water splashing over the rocks. The river seemed high and I knew it was spring.

I baited the hook and paused to study the river. I made a smooth cast. I felt a strike and flicked up the tip of my pole to hook the trout. He was all fight from the start, and I played him back and forth into the shallows where I landed him. Then I waded in and felt the ice cold water seep into my gym shoes.

Casting was easy now. I felt a sharp tug and had another battle on my hands. I worked the trout in close, hooked a finger through his gills, and slipped him into my fishing bag. I waded out farther and caught several more trout. They were full of fight and all good eating size.

The gray light of dawn showed through the mist. I started upstream and saw the good places to fish.

I waded around clumps of brush and took my time to make each cast perfect. The way was difficult, but the fishing was good.

I stopped by a roaring rapids and dropped my fishing bag in shallow water to cool the trout. Sunlight was beginning to hit the tops of the tall trees which reached branches high above the river. I looked around and felt the hair rise on the back of my neck. I had found a magic place.

I stood transfixed. A fine mist lingered in the gray shadows. The cool motionless veil draped the columns of trees and hung in the broad limbs which vaulted the ceiling above me. The stained glass patterns of leaves glowed green and gold, and a few slender shafts of sunlight angled down and turned to silver in soft diffusion. The place was full of sound, but I heard its awesome silence. I stood in a strange cathedral and knew the meaning of time without end. I felt as nothing. I was alone and the whole world started to fall away. I knew the secret of this magic place; and the secret was safe with me, for I would never be able to explain the unexplainable.

I shivered as I picked up my fishing bag and started up the rapids. I caught more trout and spent some time at the Bend where I landed a couple of beauties. Then I worked the long stretch of water that curved under the highway bridge.

The morning sun rose high above the ridge, and I stopped to count my catch. I found a grassy spot and laid the trout neatly in a row. They sparkled in the sun, and the rainbow colors dazzled my eyes.

A vague form materialized in front of me.

"Holy mackerel! You haven't moved a muscle," Dunnigan said.

"Those trout are beautiful the way they sparkle in the sun," I said.

"What? Where?" Dunnigan looked around. "What in the world are you talking about, Collins?"

"There're seventeen," I said. "If I keep moving up river, I'll have a limit before noon."

"Are you crazy?" Dunnigan asked. "Do you know you've been sitting there like that for three hours?"

"Is that all? I will have to learn to do better than that." I jumped down from the wall. "Well, let's get going."

"I still think you're some kind of nut," Dunnigan said.

32

I wasn't far from the city pool now, and I quickened my stride. The air was very hot. The mountain sky was crystal blue, and the sun was bearing straight down. I started to think ahead to the cool water of the pool.

"First I will do some diving," I said to myself. "I need to work on my front one-and-a-half."

As I rounded the last curve before the highway bridge, I started to jog. Halfway across the bridge I stopped a moment to look down. I was high above the river.

The river was low, but I knew there were still plenty of trout. I studied a few spots and figured how I would fish them. I looked down at the Bend, but nobody was there. The place didn't look so big to me anymore, and everybody swam at the city pool since it had opened.

I happened to glance at the road that came up

around the Bend to the highway, and spotted Sanchez on his way to swimming. I yelled and waved
at him, and he waved back. I jogged on across the
bridge and waited a moment as Sanchez came walking up to meet me.

"Hey, Pancho, we're getting an early start."

"Yeah, it sure is hot."

"It's a great day for swimming."

"It'll be hot all day and all night, that's for sure,"
Sanchez said.

"Well, let's get going."

We jogged across the highway and kept on jogging up alongside it. Our feet were crunching in the
gravel, and we were matching stride for stride. The
swimming pool was just beyond the Corral Bar and
Dance Hall. We could see the sign on the front of
the Corral, and we quickened our pace. We started
kicking up dust and gravel, and the race was on.

Sanchez went into his sprint. He wasn't going to
let me save anything for a kick at the end. We were
side by side going as fast as we could, but it was
hard to keep our footing on the slippery gravel. We
went flying past the Corral together, and we slid
and churned our legs as we turned up the gravel
road that led back to the entrance of the pool. The
race wasn't over yet. We were still neck and neck.

Coach Reginato was just sitting down at his little
table by the gate. He was getting ready to check

people into the pool. He looked up as he heard us come sprinting pell-mell up the road toward him. Coach Reginato jumped to his feet and waved his arms.

"Hold it! Hold it!" he yelled, but he was too late to stop us.

I came sliding up and had to grab hold of the gate post to keep from sliding under the table. Sanchez went sliding by on the other side of me and just managed to keep his feet. Coach Reginato was angry.

"Didn't you hear me?"

"Sorry, Coach, but did you see who won?" I asked.

"Are you crazy, Collins? It's too hot for this sort of thing. It's bad enough I have to sit here in the heat without you guys running up here and raising a cloud of dust." He waved his hands in the dusty air.

"We didn't mean to, Coach," Sanchez said.

"Don't you guys know you can get hurt sprinting like that on a gravel road?"

"Aw, Coach, we got to live a little."

"Collins, when are you ever going to get serious? You know you can't be so crazy all the time and get away with it."

"I thought all great athletes were supposed to be a little crazy."

"Well, in that case, you take the cake, you do.

Both you guys are going to spend a long time in the shower before I let you in the pool."

"Aw, Coach," Sanchez said.

"You're both covered with dirt from head to foot, aren't you?"

"Yes, Coach." Then Coach Reginato passed us through and gave us baskets to put our clothes in.

"Next time maybe you guys will remember this isn't the finish line."

"Okay, Coach." We went to change into our trunks. Sanchez and I spent a long time in the shower.

"Man, this water's cold," I said.

"Yeah," Sanchez said. "We must be clean by now."

"Hey, Coach!" I yelled. Finally Coach Reginato waved us into the pool.

"No running!" he yelled just in time to stop us from sprinting for the deep end. We walked as fast as we could and dove into the deep water.

"Hey, this water feels great after a cold shower," Sanchez said.

"Yeah." Together we pushed off the wall and swam across the pool and back.

"This is great," Sanchez said.

"I'm going to work on my diving before it gets too crowded."

"Okay, I think I'll do some underwater swimming."

We got out of the pool. Sanchez took a couple of deep breaths and did a long deep dive into the water and started to swim across the pool underwater. I went over to the diving board and practiced my approach a few times.

I did some jackknife dives to warm up and see how high I could get. Finally I did some front flips and started to work myself up to doing my front one-and-a-half. I did a couple, but they were a little scary. I just barely had time to see the water before I had to duck my head. I climbed out of the pool after a pretty good one-and-a-half, and I saw Dunnigan coming up the road.

"Hey, Dunnigan!" I yelled. "The water's great."

Dunnigan waved at me, and he broke into a jog as he rounded the corner at the Corral. I watched him running up the gravel road to the pool entrance.

"Oh, no," I said to myself. "Coach won't like that."

When Dunnigan finally got into the pool, he splashed around for a while. Then he and Sanchez came over to do some diving.

"What's the matter with Coach today?" Dunnigan asked.

"Hah!" Sanchez laughed.

"Pancho and I had a race to the gate," I said. "We ended in a dead heat and a cloud of dust."

"Oh, no wonder," Dunnigan said. "You guys set me up pretty good."

"Yeah, but doesn't the water feel great after a long cold shower?" Sanchez asked.

"Thanks a lot," Dunnigan said.

We did some more swimming and diving, and finally we stretched ourselves out on the hot cement and baked ourselves dry.

33

"Hey, this deck is hot," Sanchez said. "I can't move, or I'll burn myself."

"Yeah, me too. I've got to cool off."

I jumped into the pool. Dunnigan and Sanchez were right after me. We splashed around and had a water fight. Then we splashed water up onto the deck to cool it. We climbed out and got comfortable again. Dunnigan leaned back against the fence and took a deep breath.

"Man, this is the life."

"Yeah," Sanchez said. "Isn't it though?"

I saw a railroad man walking alongside the highway. He stopped to watch the kids swimming. I figured he was on his way home from a run. He carried his traveling bag and lantern in one hand. His hat was pushed far back on his head, and he was sweating. I could see the streaks of grime on his face.

"Just think," I said. "Some people don't get to go swimming."

"Yeah, people have other things they got to do," Sanchez said.

"How can they stand it?" I wondered. "They must not know what they're missing."

"Aw, everybody's gone swimming one time or another," Dunnigan said.

"I can't imagine not going swimming," I said.

"You might have to do something else someday," Dunnigan said.

"Well, I won't think about it."

I jumped up and dove into the pool. I pulled a long underwater stroke and felt my body glide through the cool water. I kept going, pushed off the opposite wall, and made it halfway back before I had to come up for air. I climbed out of the pool and stretched out on the warm cement to catch my breath.

"That was pretty good," Sanchez said.

"Thanks," I said.

A lot of kids were splashing in the pool, and people were stepping over me. I scooted over to the fence and leaned up against it with Sanchez and Dunnigan.

"It sure is hot," Dunnigan said, "and it's going to be hot again tonight."

"Yeah," Sanchez said. "Hey, did you see that moon out last night?"

"Yeah, wasn't that bright? Did you see it, Collins?"

"No, I didn't go out last night."

"Oh, it was beautiful," Dunnigan said, "and it was hot enough to go swimming."

We stopped and just looked at one another for a long moment. We didn't have to say anything to know that we were all thinking of the same thing.

"Now there's an idea," I said.

"Yeah." Sanchez rubbed his chin.

"It'll be a full moon tonight," Dunnigan said.

"Won't be any trouble climbing over this fence." Sanchez looked back over his shoulder to make sure. "If we can all get out of the house, we can sneak up here for a midnight swim."

"I can get out my bedroom window easy," Dunnigan said. "How about you, Collins?"

"I can make it. Let's plan on it."

We hit the water again and started to play a game of tag, but we had to give it up. The pool was

153

crowded, and there was a long line at the diving board. We went back to our place by the fence and got plenty of sun.

We were in and out of the pool all afternoon to cool off. At last the sun hung low over the ridge, and people started to leave. Then we started doing a lot of swimming, and I got in a good session of diving before it was time to leave. Dunnigan and I walked along with Sanchez down to his house. We stopped under a big tree right across the road.

"I'll get out of the house around eleven," I said. "Then I'll go down and tap on Dunnigan's window."

"Don't tap too loud."

"I can meet you guys right here under this tree," Sanchez said.

"Good idea. If you're not here when we get here, I'll give the hoot owl call." I folded my fingers and blew through my thumbs to make the hooting sound. "Then you'll know we're here."

"I got it," Sanchez said.

"Okay, we'll see you later."

Sanchez jogged across the road and up his front stairs. Then I walked with Dunnigan down to his place, and we said good-bye. I continued down to the swinging footbridge just below Dunnigan's house and crossed over to the yards. I was careful crossing the yards and climbed the hill to home.

Supper was good, and I was about as hungry as I could get. Father had gotten in earlier. After the dishes were done, he and Mother sat in the kitchen and talked. I went in the living room to listen to the stereo. I was hoping that everybody would get to bed early, but the time dragged on, and the night felt too hot for sleeping. Finally Mother started to put Thor to bed.

"I don't want to go to bed," Thor said. "It's too hot in there."

"It's just as hot out here. You're tired, and you have to go to bed."

"No, I'm just hot. I can't sleep it's so hot."

"Now, Thor," Mother said. "I have a nice cool sheet for you. All you'll need is just one sheet over you, and you'll see how cool it is." Mother hustled Thor into our bedroom, and I could hear her talking him into bed. Then she had him say his prayers. Thor was down for the night.

I listened to another record before Father went to take his bath. Mother told me I should go to bed. I wanted to listen to one more record, but Mother said everyone was going to bed and the stereo would be a bother, especially on a hot night. I let Mother talk me into going to bed. I went into the bedroom and found that Thor was still awake.

"You want to talk?" he asked.

"No, I don't want to talk." I stepped out of my clothes and left them on the floor where I could step right back into them.

"It's hot. How hot it got to get before you die?"

"Don't worry about it. It isn't going to get that hot." I got into bed and pulled a sheet up over me.

"I bet it could too get that hot."

"Go to sleep. Can't you see I want to go to sleep? I'm all tired out from swimming."

"I want to go swimming. You got to teach me swimming."

"You're too little."

"I am not. I can do swimming if you teach me."

"Maybe so, but you'll be a lot easier to teach when you're seven or eight."

"I want to do it now."

"I couldn't even swim much until I was nine or ten. You're better off just playing in the sprinkler."

"Aw, that's no fun."

Thor kept on talking, but I wouldn't answer him. I just lay there and waited for him to calm down. Not long after he stopped talking, I heard the slow and easy sound of his breathing. He was falling asleep.

34

I listened to Mother and Father getting ready for bed. Thor sighed a few times. Then the lights clicked off, and I heard Mother and Father get into bed. Their bedroom was just on the other side of the bathroom with a short hall between their room and ours. They must have left their door open, because I could hear them talking softly.

I listened to the pleasant sound of Mother's voice and the easy murmur of Father's deeper tones. They talked for a long time, and the night seemed calm and peaceful. I could almost make out the words, but I didn't really care to. I just liked the sound of it. I did listen just enough to hear my name mentioned a few times in some nice way.

I felt happy. I just lay there with my hands behind my head and enjoyed a feeling of belonging. I thought about saying my prayers but knew I wasn't going to sleep. Mother and Father stopped talking, and I waited.

At last I heard the low sounds of Father snoring. I knew that Mother had fallen asleep, because she didn't make him turn over. I sat up quietly.

The window by my bed was already open wide. I reached over and unhooked the window screen. I leaned out the window to look at the warm silver night. The full moon was rising above the far ridge. I took a deep breath and felt my body come alive. There was excitement in the air.

I leaned back in and turned to reach my feet to the floor. I found my Levis, stepped into them, and stood up quietly as I pulled them on. I sat back down and put on my socks and gym shoes. I slipped on an old shirt and was set to go.

I climbed softly onto my bed, pushed open the window screen, and slowly stretched a leg out the window. I stepped onto the garage roof and ducked my head and shoulders out under the screen without making any noise. I pulled my other leg free and was careful not to let the screen bang as I eased it back into place.

I crawled to the edge of the roof and climbed onto the big limb of the black walnut tree. I swung down and dropped gently to the ground. I paused to listen, but all was silence. The houses were all dark under the silver brightness. I tiptoed across the gravel driveway, walked the dirt road around the Ward place, and hurried down the path to the yards. I could see my way as plain as day.

Nothing was happening in the yards, and I crossed them quickly. The swinging footbridge was in dark shadows, and I started across slowly. The noise of the river seemed loud. I stopped and looked down, but all was blackness. The bridge swayed, and I imagined I was swinging over a black pit and the darkness was roaring up at me. I hurried across to the road.

I was on asphalt now and broke into a run. The warm night air was a joy to breathe. I turned on some speed and went sailing through the silver shadows. I slowed to a walk in front of Dunnigan's house. The lights were out. I looked all around and then walked silently up the driveway to the corner of the garage.

I studied Dunnigan's bedroom window and crept up to it. I tapped on the glass and waited. A minute went by, and I tapped again. This time the shade fluttered, and I knew Dunnigan had heard me. I crept back to the corner of the garage and waited.

After several minutes I saw the window slowly open. Without making a sound Dunnigan eased himself out the window and onto the walk. He spotted me by the garage and tiptoed over. We walked quietly down the driveway to the road.

"I told you not to tap so loud."

"I'm sorry. I didn't think you heard me."

"I had to wait to see if everybody was still asleep before I could come out."

We started jogging up the road. We ran pretty fast for a long stretch, and then we slowed to a walk. After we caught our breath, we talked about what a great night it was. When we got to the spot where we were supposed to meet Sanchez, he wasn't there. His house was dark.

I folded my fingers and blew through my thumbs to make the hoot owl call. I made a couple of loud ones. Then Dunnigan tried a few calls, and I started again. Sanchez walked up behind us.

"Are you guys trying to wake everybody up?"

"Huh, where were you?"

"I was just sitting on a rock down by the river and waiting for you."

"Oh, how late are we?"

"I don't know. I've been out for a while. What time is it?"

"I didn't bring my watch," Dunnigan said.

"Glory be," I said. "You didn't bring your watch."

"Well, you're the one who always knows what time it is."

"Hah!" Sanchez laughed. "That's right, Collins, we're on your time now."

"Well, you can tell it's coming on the middle of the night. Just look at the moon."

"Anyhow we all got out just like we planned," Dunnigan said. "What say we go for a midnight swim?"

We were off jogging up the road alongside the river. The water bubbled and sang in the rapids, and the silver moonlight glistened everywhere. Then the road started up around the Bend, and we slowed to a walk. The highway bridge looked like a misty span, and the river sparkled below us. When we got up to the highway, we stopped for a minute as a few cars cruised by.

"Some traffic on the road tonight," I said.

"Yeah, it's Friday night," Sanchez said. "I guess some people are out."

"Aw, nobody's going to pay any mind to us," Dunnigan said.

"Probably a lot of people up to the Corral," Sanchez said.

35

We sprinted across the highway and jogged alongside it until we could angle in on a side road. We slowed to a walk and went by a few dark houses. We wended our way toward the back of the Corral where the dance hall stretched out behind the bar.

As we approached, we could hear the band playing a fast number. We stopped right behind the dance hall, and the music was so loud it seemed to be vibrating the back wall. A lot of cases of empty bottles were stacked up there under a high transom-like window.

"I think I'll take a look," Sanchez said. He climbed up on the cases until he could peek in. "Man, are they ever jumping around."

Dunnigan and I climbed up on either side of him. We peeked in. The band was thumping and banging while a lot of couples were dancing madly to the heavy beat.

"Hey, there's Mary Lee," Dunnigan said.

"I sure would like to do some jumping around with her," Sanchez said.

"Doesn't she look good?" Dunnigan asked.

"Yeah, I've got to learn to dance," Sanchez said. "That's really something."

"Aw, that's nothing," I said. "That's not even dancing."

"Are you kidding?" Sanchez turned his head to look at me. "You mean you wouldn't like to jump around with Mary Lee, Collins?"

"Well, I don't have time for girls. I've got more important things to do."

"Like what?"

"Like fishing and swimming, that's what."

"Hah! You can still do all that stuff."

"You get going with girls, and you'll see. You won't get to do anything else. Besides, we got plenty of time for girls."

"Yeah, but I wish I was in there right now." Sanchez peeked in the window again.

"Well, get it out of your mind," I said. "It can't do you any good."

"Man alive, did you see the way her dress flew up?" Dunnigan asked.

"Yeah," Sanchez said. "Isn't she pretty though?"

"We don't have time to watch dancing. Let's get

going." I climbed down. "Come on . . . let's go."

"Oh, all right," Dunnigan said. "Come on, Pancho."

"That's not like a silly school dance." Sanchez took one last look and climbed down.

"Yeah, they're having fun," Dunnigan said.

"Mark my words," I said. "When you start messing with girls, you'll start trying to act all grown up. Then you'll start drinking beer and smoking cigarettes, and that'll be the end of everything."

"I don't think I'd mind doing a little bit of it. How about you, Pancho?"

"Hah! I can hardly wait."

"I thought we were going for a swim," I said.

"Okay, let's go," Dunnigan said.

We started to tiptoe along the gravel side road next to the swimming pool. A lot of cars were parked there. I saw some movement and stopped in my tracks about ten feet behind one of the cars.

"Hey," I whispered. "There's somebody in the back of that car."

We edged up a little closer and tried to see through the back window. Sanchez put a finger to his lips, and we crept around the front end of the pool.

"Hey, Pancho," I whispered. "Was that one person or two?"

"Don't be silly, Collins. What do you think?"

"I guess it was two."

"Hey, Dunnigan, did you hear that?"

"It was kind of hard to tell." Dunnigan snickered under his breath.

We went around to the fence and climbed over. The moon was straight overhead, and the pool was drenched in misty brightness. We started to undress.

"You think anybody'll see us?" I asked.

"I don't think they'll care," Sanchez said.

"Yeah," Dunnigan said, "but we better not splash around too much."

"I'll practice my silent swimming," I said.

We could still hear the band playing, and suddenly the music sounded louder as a side door of the dance hall was opened. A couple stepped out.

"I got a bottle in the car," the man said, and the woman giggled. Their footsteps crunched in the gravel as they hugged and ran laughing to his car. We finished getting undressed and eased ourselves into the water.

"Hey, this water feels great," I whispered.

"Yeah," Dunnigan said.

"I'm going to swim across underwater." Sanchez ducked out of sight.

Dunnigan and I started our silent swimming across the pool. Sanchez made it first. The side of the pool was several feet higher than the road. We hunched up on the edge of the pool to look down at the dance hall. The side door was still open. Another couple came out and went to their car, and a couple got out of their car and went back into the dance hall.

"There's more going on out here than there is in there," Sanchez whispered.

"Yeah," Dunnigan said. "We better be quiet." We did some more swimming and met again over by our clothes.

"We can't do much here," I said. "Sure can't do any diving."

"Yeah, let's go," Sanchez said. We got out of the pool, brushed the water off as best we could, and got dressed.

"I'm wet," Dunnigan said.

"We can go for a run," I said. "We'll dry off in nothing flat." We climbed back over the fence.

"Hey, I got an idea," Sanchez said. "Let's go down to the city park and see if anybody's down there."

Dunnigan liked the idea, but I didn't see any point to it.

"Nobody'd be down there," I said.

"People park down there by the river," Sanchez said.

"Bound to be somebody down there on a night like this," Dunnigan said.

"I don't know."

"What's the matter, Collins?" Sanchez asked. "Are you scared?"

"I just think it's a waste of time, that's all."

"Well, come on," Dunnigan said.

We started off jogging and went up the road alongside the ball park. We followed the road around to the top of the hill and slowed to a walk.

"Now keep your eyes open," Sanchez whispered. "We don't want them seeing us before we see them."

"Yeah," Dunnigan said. "Let's be ready to get off this road."

36

"Hey, here's the path," I said. "We can go straight down."

"Okay, but be quiet," Sanchez whispered.

The path was a short cut. The road angled down on our left to the bottom of the hill and then made a sharp turn up into the park where there were picnic tables, a set of swings and a big teeter-totter.

At the bottom of the path we stopped for a moment. We were in amongst a lot of big trees, and their branches reached high overhead. Dark shadows were all around us, but enough moonlight filtered through for us to see clearly as we made our way slowly across the park.

Then Sanchez stopped and held up a hand. He pointed at a car that was parked near the river. The car was next to some trees, but its light-colored roof shone smoothly in the bright moonlight.

"See . . . what did I tell you?"

"Yeah," I whispered. "That's a nice spot to look down at the river."

"Hey, Collins," Dunnigan whispered. "Let's give them the hoot owl call. That'll scare them."

"Wait a minute. If you want to scare them, let's do it right. How about we stalk right up behind the car. Then all at once we yell like wild Indians and pound on the fenders."

"Well, I don't know about doing all that," Sanchez whispered.

"Now who's afraid?"

"Well, okay," Sanchez whispered, "but are you sure we can make it?"

"Sure," I whispered. "Come on."

The car was headed in toward the river, so we kept to the dark shadows and easily worked our way to a spot several yards to the rear of the car. Then we got down low and started to take one quiet step at a time. Above the murmur of the river we could hear the sound of voices. There seemed to be two couples in the car. They were having a good time. Several times the men laughed, and the women giggled.

We crept very slowly until we were right up against the back bumper. I stood up a little and raised a hand. Dunnigan and Sanchez were on either side of me. I looked from one to the other to make sure they were ready.

All at once I gave a bloodcurdling cry and banged down several times on the trunk. Dunnigan and Sanchez yelled and pounded on the fenders. Then we jumped up and started to run.

I heard a car door click and open, but I was already into my sprint straight down the middle of the gravel road. Dunnigan and Sanchez were right on my heels. The car door slammed, and then the engine started up. I cut straight into the dark shadows of the park and had to keep my eyes wide open to keep from running into any trees.

I heard the car go into gear and the wheels spin as the car pulled onto the road. Dunnigan and Sanchez were breathing down my neck. I went scrambling up the hillside and hit the road again a good distance above the sharp curve. I saw that the car hadn't started into the curve yet, and I didn't hesitate an instant. I sprinted straight across the road and plunged into the dense brush on the hillside above.

I stumbled and jumped to keep my feet. I lunged ahead, took high running steps, and bounded through the chest-high branches. I could hear Dunnigan and Sanchez thrashing along behind me.

I charged ahead for a few more steps and dove headfirst into a big thicket. I bounced through the outstretched branches and hit the ground. Dunnigan and Sanchez piled in right on top of me. We just had time to get flat on the ground before the car came roaring up the hillside.

Some light from the headlights filtered through to us as the car flashed by. We waited and listened as the car sped out of the park. Things got quiet again, and we started to breathe easier.

"Hey," Dunnigan said. "I think we made them mad."

"I looked back just when we started to run," Sanchez said, "and I think I recognized one of those Hoeber boys. If he catches us, he'll skin us alive."

"I don't like the sound of that," Dunnigan said. "What do you think, Collins?"

"Oh, I don't know."

"I mean do you think they'll try to catch us?"

"Yeah, they might try to," I said. "They've got to be pretty mad all right. I bet they'd like to get their hands on us."

"Well, come on," Dunnigan said. "Let's get going."

"No . . . just sit down and get comfortable."

"Huh?" Dunnigan asked, but he sat back down.

"We must use the wisdom of the quail."

"How's that again?" Sanchez asked.

"We must be as the quail and stay right here and not move," I said. "Nobody's going to come through all this brush just on the chance we might be here. No, they'll try to catch us out in the open."

"You think so?" Dunnigan asked.

"Yeah, they might be sitting somewhere right now waiting for us to show ourselves."

"I never thought of that."

"Yeah, if that Hoeber spots us wandering around here, he'll put two and two together," Sanchez said.

"Well, how long are we going to be quail?" Dunnigan asked. "I'm not going to sit in this bush all night."

"Let's just take it easy for a while," I said. "I'll think of something."

"How did we get in this mess anyhow?"

"What always happens when Collins gets us pretending we're Indians or animals or something like that?" Sanchez asked.

"Yeah, that's right," Dunnigan said. "I shouldn't have asked. We always end up doing something crazy. Actually this isn't so bad. You wouldn't think that laying in the brush would be so comfortable."

"Yeah, but we're going to be too old for this sort of thing pretty soon," Sanchez said.

"Aw, we got plenty of time."

"Well, we've got to decide what we're going to do when we grow up," Dunnigan said.

"Those teachers have been telling us that bunk for years," I said.

"Yeah, but it's going to happen sooner or later," Sanchez said.

"So let it happen."

"What're you going to do when you grow up, Pancho?" Dunnigan asked.

"Well, after I go to college, I'm going to get me a good steady job. Then I figure I'll get into some kind of business."

"That sounds good. I'm going to try for a degree in electrical engineering."

"That figures," I said. "I can just see you working on all those fancy new gadgets."

"Well, it's an up and coming field," Dunnigan said.

"What're you going to do, Collins?" Sanchez asked.

"I don't know. I'll think about it when the time comes."

"But we all have to plan for the future," Dunnigan said.

"It doesn't matter what I do. I just want to be great, that's all."

"Hah! You don't want much, do you?" Sanchez asked.

"I don't think we can all plan on being great," Dunnigan said.

"Why not? Isn't there some kind of greatness in everybody?"

"Well, I guess that's true in a way," Dunnigan said.

"I see greatness in both of you, and I want the same thing for you guys that I want for myself."

"That sounds fair," Sanchez said.

"And haven't we already done a lot of great things?"

"Sure," Sanchez said.

"So why should it be any different in the future?"

"I don't know about all that," Dunnigan said. "I'll have to think about it."

37

The low sound of a car engine startled us. We stopped talking and looked at one another as we listened. The sound got louder, and we could hear the tires on the dirt road as the car eased down into the park, but we couldn't see any light from the headlights.

We stood up a little to take a look as the car went by us and started into the sharp curve at the bottom of the hill. Suddenly the lights flashed on, and the engine roared as the car sped into the park. The rear wheels churned up the gravel, and the car was swung in a big circle. The headlights swept through the dark shadows like two searchlights.

Then the car headed back and roared into the sharp curve. We hit the dirt as the car flashed by us and went up out of the park. We were quiet for a moment and listened to the fading sound of the car.

"Holy mackerel," Dunnigan whispered.

"You sure were right, Collins," Sanchez said. "They're trying to catch us out in the open."

"Yeah, they're pretty smart all right but not smart enough to catch us."

"Yeah, but how're we going to get out of here?" Dunnigan asked.

"That's no problem. I can guarantee we get back to town and nobody'll even come close to seeing us. We won't have to worry about a thing."

"Well, what's the plan?" Dunnigan asked.

"Since we don't want to take any chances, we

stick to the brush and work our way down to the river. It's not very far. I fished the river around here a whole lot, and I know a spot a little way down where it's real easy to cross. We won't get wet much above our knees. Then we climb up to the tracks and walk them back to town."

"I don't know," Dunnigan said. "What do you think, Pancho?"

"Sounds pretty good to me. I sure don't want that Hoeber catching sight of me anywhere around here. He's liable to recognize me."

"Okay, I'm game," Dunnigan said. "You lead the way, Collins." We stood up quietly, and I looked around to get my bearings.

"We've got plenty of time, so let's take it easy," I said. "Stick close together, and keep your ears open."

I pushed through the brush and started to angle down off the hillside. Dunnigan had a hold on my shirt, and Sanchez had a hold on him. In a few minutes we hit the river and waded right in.

"Well, that wasn't so bad," Dunnigan said.

"Hey, the water's hardly cold," I said, "but watch your step. These rocks are real mossy this time of year."

"Hey, you're right." Sanchez slipped and had to take a quick step to catch his balance.

"Easy does it," Dunnigan said. We walked along

the edge of the river down to a wide place where the water flowed out smoothly just above some rapids.

"Here's the spot," I said.

"Looks pretty far," Dunnigan said.

"Yeah, but it's shallow, and the water isn't moving too fast."

"Well, let's get going," Sanchez said.

I started across and felt my way along with my feet. The rocks were slippery. Dunnigan grabbed hold of my belt and held out his other arm for Sanchez to grab onto.

"Hang on," Dunnigan said, "and take it easy."

"How do you keep your feet out here?" Sanchez asked.

"Get both feet planted solid before you take the next step," I said.

I took one step at a time and waited for Dunnigan and Sanchez to take a step. We inched out into the middle of the river and started for the other side. The water was over our knees here and moving faster into the rapids.

"Hold it up," Sanchez said. "I've got to get my feet set."

I just stood there and looked about me. I felt the cool water pushing hard against my legs and making my knees wobble. I listened to the river, and the murmuring sounds seemed to rush against my ears.

The moonlight glistened everywhere, and silver sparkles seemed to go dancing down the river. I took a deep breath and tasted the cool breeze. A beautiful feeling came over me.

"This is a magic place," I said. "Just look at the river."

"Well, let's get across it," Dunnigan said.

"My foot's not set," Sanchez said.

"You see that boulder up there? I caught some nice trout right behind it. That was a long time ago on the first opening day I ever fished. No wonder this is a magic place."

"Come on," Dunnigan said. "Let's move."

"Hold it!" Sanchez yelled.

Then he started splashing around to keep his balance, but he went down. Dunnigan held on to him and jerked my belt. I started to fall backward. I swung my arms to stay upright, but there was another tug at my belt, and I slowly flopped straight back into the river.

I felt a big splash. The current swept me against Dunnigan, and he tumbled down. The three of us were hanging on to one another and splashing around trying to get to our feet. We bounced along over the slippery rocks and floated into the rapids. Dunnigan was sputtering.

"You did it again, Collins. You did it again!" he yelled. "You and your magic place!"

"Well, stop yelling, and let's get across!" I yelled.

We rode the rapids until Sanchez finally grabbed on to a rock. Dunnigan and I were swept around behind him into the calm water. The three of us managed to stand up and get out of the river. Dunnigan was still sputtering.

"I should've known something like this was going to happen!" he yelled. "Something like this always happens. Look at us. We're soaked!"

"Hah!" Sanchez laughed. "That was sure some ride in the dark."

"Well, let's get up to the tracks," I said.

We stumbled around and finally managed to climb up to the tracks. We started walking slowly toward town. We were still dripping wet, and our shoes squished with every step.

"What a mess," Dunnigan said. "I'm all wet. I'm muddy. I'm starting to get cold, and it's a long walk back."

"Yeah," Sanchez said.

"Pancho, how come every time we do something with Collins, it always ends up like this?" Dunnigan asked.

"I don't know, but come to think about it, you're right. We've had some wild times."

"Yeah, but I've got to admit they don't seem so bad after they've happened," Dunnigan said. "In fact, they're fun to remember and talk about; but while they're happening, I feel miserable."

"Yeah, that's funny all right," Sanchez said.

"Oh, I don't know," I said. "If things were nice and easy, they wouldn't be worth remembering."

"Well, with you around we'll never have to worry about that," Dunnigan said.

"Yeah," Sanchez said. "We always get something to remember."

38

We walked around a big curve, and the steel rails glistened in the moonlight. Dunnigan started talking about some of the crazy things we had done together, and pretty soon we were all remembering and talking about them. Sanchez laughed a few times, and Dunnigan was back in a cheerful mood.

"Wait a minute," Dunnigan said. "What am I laughing about? I'm all wet. I can't go home like this. What're we going to do?"

"Let's just keep going," I said.

"Keep going?"

"Sure, we'll dry off sooner or later."

"I can't think of anything else to do," Sanchez said.

We walked along and passed under the highway bridge. After we got around the next big curve, we could see a few lights down at the roundhouse.

"Not much doing tonight," Dunnigan said.

"Pretty quiet," Sanchez said.

When we got down by the depot, we started to jog. We headed up to the street and on down past the yard office. We still sounded wet as we ran, but nobody was around. We jogged up the hill and ran down the road to where it crossed the tracks.

"Let's keep going," I said, and we stepped up the pace all the way down to the street bridge that crossed the river above Dunnigan's house. We walked to catch our breath.

"I'm still wet," Dunnigan said.

"Yeah, but we lost some of our squish," I said.

"Hah!" Sanchez laughed. "But now I'm working up a sweat." We walked past Dunnigan's house and on down past the swinging footbridge. The river road stretched out before us.

"Let's just run half-speed," I said, "and see how far we get before we dry off."

We started off nice and easy and matched stride for stride. Our feet patted the smooth asphalt with a steady beat that sounded nice against the background of the murmuring river. The air tasted sweet. I took a deep breath and let it out.

"Man alive, I could run like this all night."

"Does feel pretty good," Sanchez said.

"Yeah, but this is the dumbest way to dry off I ever heard of," Dunnigan said.

We ran a long way in silence. The road was dusted with patches of silver, and the cool mountain air was scented with all the fresh fragrances that would haunt the morning dew. I thought that a great force was bidding us on and on. All was movement, running legs, and swinging arms. A voice sang from our lungs. We were alive, and life was a celebration.

"It's getting dark," Sanchez said, and we slowed to a walk.

"Yeah, the moon's going down," Dunnigan said.

"Man, that was a great run." I took a deep breath and let it out slowly. Dunnigan started to laugh.

"Hey, it worked," he said. "I'm just about dry."

"Me too," Sanchez said. "How about that?"

"Well, we might as well start back."

"Yeah, I'm about wore out," Dunnigan said.

We turned around and started back. After we felt rested again, we jogged a little bit. Then we just walked. Sanchez tilted his head back and looked up.

"The sky looks a little lighter."

"Yeah," I said. "It'll be dawn pretty soon."

"Holy mackerel, we've been out all night."

"Looks that way," Sanchez said. "You guys going swimming today?"

"Sure," I said. "We can lay around the pool and rest up."

"Good idea," Dunnigan said.

We walked quietly for a time as if we were lost in our own thoughts. Even the river seemed to be talking softly to itself. When we got to the swinging footbridge, we stopped.

"Well, it's been fun," I said.

"Yeah," Sanchez said. "It was a real interesting night."

"It was wet," Dunnigan said.

"Just look at that sky. You can see the night still hanging there. It's like that when time stands still."

"That's hardly possible, Collins," Dunnigan said.

"I believe time can stand still. I believe you can grab a moment like this one and hold it in your hand." I reached out and closed my hand and held it for Dunnigan and Sanchez to see.

"Is that all there is to it?" Sanchez asked.

"Well, because of the nature of things, you have to open your hand and let the moment slip away." I opened my hand slowly.

"Is it gone?" Sanchez looked at my hand.

"You don't lose all of it. You still have the part

that's like the dust off a butterfly's wing. That part you carry with you for all the rest of your life."

"Hey, that sounds nice," Sanchez said.

"I never heard such hogwash before," Dunnigan said. "Why is it, Collins, that about the time I get used to one of your nutty ideas, you come up with one that's even nuttier?"

"Hah! Sounds like Socrates should've been with us tonight."

"Yeah," I said. "I bet he would've liked to ride those rapids in the moonlight."

"We would've soaked him good," Sanchez said.

"Oh, for Pete's sake," Dunnigan said. "I'm too tired for this. We better all get home and get some sleep."

"Yeah, I'll probably sleep a little late," I said, "but I'll see you guys at the pool."

"Okay," Dunnigan said.

"Yeah, take it easy," Sanchez said.

We parted, and I waved as I started across the swinging footbridge. I suddenly felt weary, but I paid attention crossing the yards. All was quietness before the dawn. My legs felt very tired as I climbed the hill to home, but I felt all alive inside.

"That's strange," I said to myself. "Sometimes being all worn out is a great feeling."

I stopped at the top of the hill and looked back.

Most of the stars had slipped away, and a bright line of light showed above the eastern ridge. I turned and walked quietly for home. Everything seemed hushed and waiting for the dawn.

I took my time climbing the black walnut tree and stepped carefully onto the garage roof. I quietly edged my way over to the bedroom window. I paused for one last look around me. I could see all the houses clearly. I felt a great silence. The night was fading to an end, and the cool light of dawn was spilling over into the canyon. I eased out the window screen and climbed softly onto my bed.

I undressed very slowly and shoved all my damp clothes under the bed where they were sure to dry out good before Mother found them. I put on a dry pair of shorts and started to get into bed. I heard Thor sigh, and then I noticed that he had fallen out of bed again. He had pulled his pillow and his sheet down with him, and he was all huddled up on the rug. I spotted a light blanket at the foot of his bed. I tiptoed over, spread out the blanket, and threw it over him.

"Looks like he's going to wake up on the floor again," I whispered to myself.

I started to turn toward my bed, but the corner of my eye caught a glimpse of something crawling near Thor's pillow. I grabbed a book off my dresser and took aim. Then I saw that the thing was only my wristwatch with one of the straps stretched out.

"It's about time," I whispered and smiled to myself.

Thor had finally found my wristwatch. No doubt he had enjoyed playing with it, and before falling asleep he had slipped it under his pillow for safekeeping. I knelt down and picked up the watch. The back of the thing was loose. I snapped it tight, and then I pushed the watch under Thor's pillow. Thor hunched up a little more and hugged his pillow, but he still slept soundly.

I got into bed and stretched out to get comfortable. After I said my prayers, I felt how tired I was. I wanted to explore all the interesting things I had thought about during the past day and night, but in the weariness of my mind I had to struggle from one idea to the next.

I was down to the river, and the way was hard with all the climbing through the brush and wading in the water. I found a sunny place and stopped to count my catch. I laid the glistening ideas neatly in a row. They sparkled in the sunlight. It had taken me some time, but I had caught me a nice mess of things to think about.

Stream Runner is David Seed's first novel. He decided to be a writer when he was in high school, and set out to get the kinds of experiences most writers seemed to have. He became a newspaper artist and printer, drove cabs, perfected the art of poker playing, and worked as a railroad brakeman. He even spent some time working in a cannery in Yakutat, Alaska. There he came to be known as the "Crazy Californian," and that was a pleasant surprise.

The author has always been an avid sportsman, with many medals for track and gymnastics. He graduated from the University of California at Berkeley with a major in physical education, and he has been a high school teacher and a sports instructor. He grew up in Dunsmuir where the trout fishing is "the best."

Today David Seed lives in Oakland, California.